A Bitter Sacrifice

A Bitter Sacrifice

Ophelia B. Sellers

New Harbor Press
RAPID CITY, SD

Sellers/New Harbor Press
1601 Mt. Rushmore Rd. Ste 3288
Rapid City, SD 57701
www.newharborpress.com

Ordering Information:
Quantity sales. Special discounts are available on quantity purchases by corporations, associations, and others. For details, contact the "Special Sales Department" at the address above.

A Bitter Sacrifice/Sellers. —1st ed.
ISBN 978-1-63357-199-0

Chapter 1

Alivia had barely unpacked her bags and was eagerly anticipating the summer ahead of her. She grinned as she thought back to her graduation ceremony two days ago, one of the most important days of her life. She had floated across that platform in a cloud of euphoria. Her entire family, including her fiancé and his family, was in attendance. Princeton had held her prisoner for four years, but that paper in her hand was the key that unlocked the cage and set her free. She was ready to fly.

Now she could complete the wedding plans with Peter. Her heart was light, and everything was right in her world—until she began the conversation with her dad.

Angrily, Alivia asked, "Dad, why didn't you tell me sooner? I could have come home." She didn't appreciate her parents keeping important news from her. She had wondered why her dad looked so serious and down and out. In her wildest dreams she couldn't have anticipated the news she had just heard.

"That is exactly why I did not tell you. Meagan and I talked it over and decided to wait until you were finished with school to let you know about her heart trouble. You would have fretted about it, and the news may have interfered with your studies. Do you think you could have concentrated on your final exams knowing your mother was seriously ill?"

"No, I couldn't have. But I still think I deserved to know that my mother has a heart defect and must have surgery in the next few weeks. I'm an adult now, Dad, not a small child. You do remember that I just graduated from Princeton, don't you? Don't feel that you must keep distressing news from me. Please allow me to process information in my own way. How am I to mature if you keep treating me like a little girl?"

With a sigh he replied, "Duly noted. I'll try my best to keep you updated from now on."

Meagan entered the room and went straight to Alivia. Arms open wide, she embraced her daughter. "Punkin, please don't be angry with us about this. It was my wish to keep this from you to spare you undue stress at a vitally important time in your life. I'm sorry if you don't agree with our decision, but we thought it best."

"I'm not angry, Mother, but it makes me feel like you still consider me too much of a baby to handle hard things. Mom. Dad. You have taught me from an early age to trust God with all my problems and concerns. Now you must allow me to fly with my own wings. I know that God will always be there to help me and give me strength."

Kenneth and Meagan exchanged sheepish looks as they both laughed and embraced her. "My grown-up daughter. I can hardly accept that you are a woman now and not just my little punkin. More than likely you will have to remind us a few more times." Meagan kissed her forehead and left the room.

Kenneth eyed his daughter as he considered his next step. He closed the door and took a deep breath before he plunged in. "Alivia, I'm glad to know you are levelheaded enough to handle trouble because I have some rather startling news. I have tentatively arranged a marriage between you and Dayne Travers. I hope—"

"What? Dad, this is not funny. If this is supposed to be a joke, you failed miserably." She waited for him to cross the room and take her by the shoulders, laugh loudly, and give her a hug. He didn't.

"Honey, I wish it were a joke, but I'm afraid it's true. Let me explain, please. I have made some bad decisions with investments and am almost broke. I am, at the least, in severe financial trouble. Dayne approached me a few weeks ago with a proposition."

Alivia couldn't wait for him to finish his speech before breaking in again. "How could your financial status matter to Dayne Travers? Who is he? Most importantly, why has my name been brought into the equation?"

"Dayne is the richest man in the state, Alivia. His specialty is buying companies that are failing and rebuilding them into profitable businesses. He has been successful with several companies that I am familiar with.

"Dayne is a highly sought-after speaker and conducts seminars and conventions teaching others how to be successful. He is a special young man, Alivia. His wealth has not ruined him, as is the case with many young men who grow up in the life of luxury. He also has a benevolent heart and supports many charities.

"He is a Christian man, Alivia, with high standards of excellence and integrity. He is a man who is worthy of trust. I have known of him for years, though not personally."

Alivia was skeptical. "If he is so wonderful why is it so difficult for him to find a wife? I still don't get the connection, Dad. What is his interest in me? I have never met the man. Why would I have any part in the negotiations between your company and him?"

Kenneth stood and placed his hands in his pockets. "As I said earlier, he approached me. He had heard that my company is in trouble and came up with a proposal. He agreed to fund my company and leave me as CEO if I agree to the marriage. As to why he is interested in you, I can't answer that question. I'm sure that in time he will explain his thoughts to you."

She expelled her breath in a huff and stood to her feet. "Dad, you know that Pete and I plan to marry within the next few months. Why should I even consider this man as a husband? Dad, what were you thinking?"

"You are the deal-breaker, Alivia. No marriage, no deal."

"What? That is crazy! Why? He doesn't even know me! This is too absurd to even contemplate. Pete will never voluntarily step down and allow me to marry someone else, money or not. We have been promised to each other for years. You already know this, Dad."

"Alivia, your mother's heart condition is critical. I can't allow her to be under such stress as she would be if our lives were turned upside down with bankruptcy. We would lose everything, including this ranch that she loves so much. There are also five hundred employees that will lose their income if my company folds."

Alivia looked at her dad in disbelief. "Dad. Is there no other way? Have you tried the banks for a loan? Don't you have money in savings? Why do I have to be the scapegoat? I feel that you are using me as chattel. Is this how you view me, Dad? As an asset to be used as a bargain tool?"

"Of course not, honey. I love you dearly. Normally I would never even consider such a deal as he has offered. This is a really hard time for us right now. The financial trouble couldn't have come at a more inconvenient time, with Meagan's health so risky."

"How long do you have before he wants a decision?"

With his head hung low, he answered, "Two weeks."

"You're kidding! I have two weeks to decide the course of my whole future? Dad, there must be some other way. I don't think I could possibly do what you're asking. I feel like you've just hit me with a sledgehammer. I'm going for a ride to clear my head. I haven't been on Shadow for a month."

Chapter 2

Alivia reveled in the freedom she felt on the back of her favorite horse. Hair flying behind her, the sun on her face, she gave Shadow her head and went along for the ride—let Shadow decide where she wanted to take her. Alivia didn't feel capable of deciding anything. She had just received a shock of a lifetime. It was all she could do to breathe.

Why should she be the one who held the life of so many people in the palm of her hand? She didn't ask for or want this position her dad had put her in. If she allowed herself to do so, she could be very angry with her dad. He was asking too much of her. What was he thinking? Her parents had always treated her with love and affection. She certainly didn't feel the love right now. How could her dad ask this of her? Could he so easily turn her life upside down to save his business? Her mind was in a fog.

What kind of man would purchase a bride? Was he an ogre, and this was the only way he can get a woman to marry him? Was he old and decrepit? Alivia thought only royalty still participated in arranged marriages. No matter how rich or handsome this man was, Alivia wanted no part of him. She had always considered marriage a sacred covenant. She had daydreamed about the day she and Pete would be married. They would work in Dallas, live close to their parents, and would have a wonderful life together. Their families would blend together as one big family and would share all aspects of life. She would live out her fairy-tale.

What was she to do? College had not prepared her for this kind of test. If she said no, would she be placing her mother at risk of dying? Alivia hated that so many people would be unemployed, but they weren't her responsibility. She felt sure they could find replacement jobs. But her mother!

Was her dad thinking rationally? Did he really believe that the consequences of his failure could be a death toll? Alivia had always looked up to her mother and thought that she was a wonder woman of strength and wisdom.

Dad had put her in an impossible position, and she didn't like it one bit. She had just left college and was about to start a new job next week. She had plans. How could her dad have put her right into the middle of the situation, a situation that she had no part in making? Her brows almost met as she considered the proposition. She couldn't—she wouldn't—do it. Before going forward with any preposterous scheme, she would consult the cardiologist and do some research online. There must be an alternate method of keeping her mother calm.

Shadow had brought them to a large pond surrounded by shade trees—an idyllic spot. The massive blue sky was a literal umbrella over the horizon, giving way to the brightness of the sun. Alivia dismounted and walked with Shadow to the edge of the water. A mother duck waddled to the water as six little ducklings waddled behind. Bees flitted all around, busy with whatever it is that bees do, probably helping to stir up the everlasting pollen that permeated the air.

Alivia stared at the water as if it should have the answer to her problem. All that was visible to her were the funny little tadpoles swimming around the edge of the pond. April was usually her favorite time of year with the Texas Bluebonnets prolific in the area. But now, even the beautiful flowers didn't bring cheer to her flagging spirits.

She looked into the huge brown eyes of her pet as she rubbed her velvety nose. "Shadow, I wish you could talk. I wonder what your advice would be. Would you willingly sacrifice your life for another? Jesus did exactly that, but then He was God. Do you think I can possibly be as selfless? Oh, Shadow, I am so confused.

"Mother has always given excellent advice, but this problem must be kept from her. Dad can't give impartial advice, and I think I know what Pete will say. I'm in a fix, Shadow."

Chapter 3

Having arrived back to the stables, Alivia still had no acceptable answer. How was she to make a life-changing decision in a matter of mere days? She handed Shadow off to one of the stable boys and headed inside.

She went straight to her room and into the shower, her mind continually circling the problem. After she finished getting dressed, she picked up her cell to call Pete. She had a lump of lead the size of Texas in her stomach.

"Hi, Pete. I just returned from a glorious ride on Shadow. She is still such a sweetheart."

Pete laughed and said, "She isn't the only sweetheart I know. I know an incredible one. One I plan to go to sleep with every night and wake up with every morning. It seems like I have waited a lifetime for you to finish college so we can be together. We must get busy with wedding plans if we expect to have things ready for a Christmas wedding. Do you still want to marry at Christmas?"

Oh no. How should she answer this question? "Pete, I have to see you and talk over a very important matter. Do you plan to come over after work this evening?"

"I thought that is what we decided yesterday. Have you forgotten me already? Hmm, I will have to think of something that will make me unforgettable. Let me see . . . "

Alivia imagined his brows going up and down and could hear the smile in his voice. Better store up the sound because after she finished the conversation with him tonight, she felt sure he wouldn't be smiling.

"Come early for dinner. Mom and Dad always like having you. I believe Mom considers you her son. Poor Mom. Only two daughters. No son."

"I will be honored to fill that spot. I can hardly wait to see you, Liv. Do you realize we haven't seen each other in a whole month? Not counting FaceTime. Soon we won't have to say goodbye to each other. I like the sound of that."

Alivia felt the noose tighten around her throat. She piddled the afternoon away, one slow hour after the other. She was waiting at the door when Pete knocked. The afternoon had offered plenty of time for her to work herself into a bundle of raw nerves. She recognized rebellion in her mind, but so far, she had not allowed it to take root in her heart.

Alivia jerked the door open and flung herself into Pete's arms, putting her heart and soul into the impromptu hug. "Wow. I like the welcome, sweetie." He held her close for several minutes, planting tiny kisses all over her face and her lips. Alivia clung to him like Velcro.

"Pete, I have missed you so much. I would swear that the last month had more than four weeks in it." Her mind wandered into forbidden territory. A place where there was no more Pete in her life. A place where a shadow stood in his place.

"I agree. At least six weeks." He smiled at her with love shining from his eyes. He had such beautiful, sparkling brown eyes. Alivia could stare into them all day. She had no desire to take the twinkle from his eyes, but she was afraid that was exactly what would happen tonight.

Dinner was a lively affair even though Alivia could not enter the frivolity with her whole heart. She dreaded what would come after dinner. Throat dry, she gulped down two glasses of water.

"Mom, dinner was great, but you won't mind if I snag Pete for myself, will you?"

With a smile she answered, "Of course not, honey."

Not wanting to chance her mother hearing their conversation, Alivia suggested they take a walk. "Pete, look up at the sky. There's a full moon and a million stars shining. Aren't the stars bigger and brighter in Texas than in any other place? God's creation is stunning, don't you think?

With eyes trained on Alivia, he said, "I agree. His creation is beautiful. Especially the one I'm looking at."

She smiled and shook her head. "I meant the sky, Peter Miller." She reached over and playfully punched him in the arm.

How could she leave him? How could she not?

With hands clasped, they began a short walk. "Pete, I have something to discuss with you. I don't quite know how to say what I need to tell you."

He stopped them and said, "Just start at the beginning, and tell me what I need to hear. But before you begin the discussion, there is one thing I feel the need to do." He cupped her face in his strong hands and placed his lips on hers in a sweet and delicious kiss.

She grasped his hands tighter. Looking anywhere but into his eyes, she said, "Pete, you know I love you. For years we have planned to marry as soon as I completed college. I want to do that, Pete. But I don't know if it will be possible."

With a frown he asked, "Why wouldn't it be possible, Liv? I haven't changed my mind. Have you? The only obstacle in our path was removed when you graduated."

"I still want to marry you, Pete, but a personal matter has developed and I don't know what to do." She slipped her hands from his and covered her face, jaws clenched to hold back tears.

"Sweetheart, listen to me. We can work through any problem you have. Tell me about it, and I will think of a way out for us. I won't allow anything to separate us, Liv."

"I know you mean that, Pete. I've always felt the same about you. I'm going to have to divulge personal things to you for you to understand."

"I'm all ears."

Taking a deep breath, she quickly spewed out the words that had to be voiced. "Dad explained to me a couple of days ago that his company is in severe financial distress. He made some investments that did not pan out like he had hoped. He is on the verge of financial ruin. His company is facing bankruptcy."

"How would that affect us, Liv? I'm very sorry for this unfortunate state of affairs, but I don't see how it can interfere with our wedding. We can have a very small wedding that won't cost him much. As a matter of fact, I'll pay all the expenses, and he won't be out any money at all."

Alivia placed her hand on his cheek. "Pete, you are such a dear. I'm afraid it is way more complicated than the cost of a wedding. Pete . . . Pete, Dad has had an offer of assistance from a man named Dayne Travers. Do you know him?"

"Sure. Everyone knows Dayne Travers. He owns multiple companies. He reminds me of a vulture, keeping his eyes open for dying companies and buying them. He is a shark, Liv. You should probably suggest to your dad that he avoid having a thing to do with the man. He makes a profit on everything he touches. Has he made an offer to your dad?"

"Yes. He has promised my dad he can retain his position of CEO and will give necessary funding. There's a stipulation, though."

"OK. I knew there must be a catch. He is not exactly the most benevolent man around from what I know. You can bet he stands to make money, or he wouldn't offer. Tell me all about it if you think I need to know."

Voice barely audible she said, "He wants me, Pete."

"What do you mean he wants you? What do you have to do with the company? Does he want you to work there with your dad?"

"No," she whispered. "He wants me to marry him."

Peter stared at Alivia in astonishment. "What? No way! I can't believe this. He can't just buy you like he does companies. Did your dad tell him you are already engaged to be married? Did he tell him that he would not give up his daughter for any amount of money? What did your dad tell him?"

"Dad agreed to let him know my answer in two weeks."

"Well, we can answer the question today. The answer is no! Of course, the answer is no."

"Pete." She looked at him beseechingly. "There is more to the story. My mother is critically ill with a heart defect and needs surgery. The cardiologist told Dad that she must not be under any stress at all before surgery. Stress will make her condition worse—maybe even cause her to die. Dad feels that if she were to find out about the financial difficulty, she may be so stressed it would kill her. Dad had our personal assets in with the company assets. If he loses the company, he also loses the ranch."

Running his hand through his hair, he puffed out, "Alivia. Can't your dad keep silent until after her surgery? Surely the defect in her heart can be corrected. Besides, you are not responsible for your parent's misfortune. I don't mean to sound unfeeling, but you can't fix this. It isn't your place to figure out your dad's dilemma. He got himself into this mess without you. Why should you give up your plans for his lack of judgment? And don't forget to count me in. My life would be ruined also. No, Alivia, no!"

Chapter 4

What a mess! What was she to do? She loved all the people involved in the issue and didn't want anyone hurt. But someone had to be hurt. Whatever decision she made would be both a blessing and a curse. Why did her dad do this to her? It was so hard! If only her life had a rewind button so that she could replay the last couple of days. She had not realized how blessed and wonderful her life had been until this disaster showed up and threatened to devastate her whole world. At the very least, her world would be changed so that her dreams would vanish with a single decision. Was it even possible to dream new dreams after her plans crashed?

Did her dad underestimate his wife's strength? Alivia had always looked to her mother as a role model. She thought her mother was the bravest, most devout Christian she knew. Would it really be possible that she could collapse by losing her home? Only God knew for sure. Did Alivia want to take a chance on her mother's health? If she said no to Dad, could she live with the guilt if the worst should happen? She could never forgive herself.

Lord, are you there? Is there another way to do this? Alivia wished God would just appear to her in her room and tell her flat out what to do, or maybe sit down at the kitchen table and share a cup of coffee. Sometimes it seemed impossible to read God. What did he want from her? She would try to do whatever He asked of her, but she had to be certain that the directive really was from God and not something her mind or another person conjured up.

She had offered herself to God recently in an especially emotional prayer time. She told Him that He could have her time, money, talent, and anything else she had. Would God really take her up on that promise? Would she have to literally sacrifice her whole future for the sake of others? Could she do it? It seemed to Alivia that Jesus giving His life would be enough for everyone and for every circumstance.

She heard the quietest whisper. "Did you mean what you said?"

"Yes, Lord. I meant it. But you're going to have to give me strength to do it. I never dreamed you would require that I actually give my life. I have all these plans with Pete, my job, my friends. Is there no other way, Lord?" Silence answered her question.

She rose to her feet and stepped to the window where she gazed at the canopy of twinkling stars, bright from the light of the full moon. It was the same glorious scene that she had viewed with Pete only moments before. Somehow the night sky had lost some of its splendor.

Closing the drapes, she turned from the window and picked up her phone to call her best friend, Morgan—the same friend she had visualized as her maid of honor. If she did follow through with her father's wishes, what would her wedding be like? Would she be able to plan any of it? If Dayne allowed her any choices, did she want to make them? How could a marriage made in such haste ever be a success? Especially when the couple did not know each other. To Alivia, the wedding seemed doomed from the start. Alivia was smart. She knew the divorce statistics of couples who were in love with each other, much less marrying a stranger.

Morgan answered immediately. "Hi, Alivia. I was talking about you only a minute ago. Lara and I wondered when we would get together to plan your wedding. We don't really have much time, you know. If you and Pete still want a Christmas wedding, we'd better get busy. Just tell me what you want me to do, and I'll get right on it. You haven't even decided on your dress or where you'll have the reception. There are a lot of decisions to make and not much time left to make them."

"About the wedding . . . there may possibly be a change in plans. I need to discuss something with you, Morgan. It is serious, and I need some good advice."

"Wow, Alivia. What's up? You and Pete aren't having trouble, are you? I mean, you and Pete are so close we can't say one of your names without the other. You two are already one."

"Yes and no. I have a dilemma that I can't seem to avoid. My dad told me some news this morning that brought me to my knees. Literally. He explained to me that Mom has a critical heart defect and will need to have open-heart surgery soon. I felt my own heart being squeezed at the news."

Alivia heard the gasp on the other end of the phone and allowed Morgan a minute to digest the news. "Mom cannot handle any kind of stress right now. The doctor explained to Dad that stress can trigger heart problems. Stress can create inflammation, triggering an increase of a hormone called cortisol. The cortisol can raise blood sugar levels and blood pressure. The overproduction of cortisol can lead to a constant state of chemical arousal, which eventually can cause a heart attack."

"Oh my goodness, Alivia. Did your dad say what the cardiologist plans to do for her? Or can they help her? With modern medical technology and all the new drugs there are, surely they can do something to save her."

"Apparently Mom must have been born with a valvular heart disease. She has had numerous tests run in the last few weeks while I was still at school, which, by the way, really bothers me. They purposely kept this news from me so I wouldn't worry about her. Can you believe it? Wouldn't you want to know if something so critical was going on with your mother's health?"

"Of course I would, Alivia. I am not ashamed to say how much I love and rely on my mother. I can't even imagine her being seriously ill. I would want to know immediately if she had a health problem. Really, Alivia, our moms trump college exams every time. We could always pick up lost credits at any time. Our mother's health should be in first place. I would be furious with my dad if he withheld that kind of information from me."

"Exactly. Poor Dad is almost out of control worried about her—he must be to bring up the solution he came up with. I'm not sure Dad would appreciate me blabbing his personal financial situation to other people, but if I don't talk to somebody I am going to implode. Have you ever heard of a man named Dayne Travers?"

"No. I don't think so. Who is he? How does he come into the picture?"

"He is a tycoon who buys small companies that are struggling and turns them into profitable businesses. He contacted Dad after getting the word that Dad is in trouble."

"What? Does the man have someone whose job is to keep a sharp eye out for companies to buy? How else would he hear about this kind of thing?"

"Morgan, believe me when I say I don't know a thing about this Dayne person. I've never heard of him before today. Help me, Morgan! I am desperate for prayer. It seems that his financial help comes with a condition. That condition is me. He insists on marrying me."

Morgan shrieked into the phone so loud that Alivia had to move it away from her ear.

"You are not serious! Tell me you aren't."

"I'm dead serious, Morgan. Dad said that the marriage is a deal-breaker. Unless I agree to marry him, he won't help my dad. I feel like I am trapped in a nightmare with no way out.

This man's mandatory condition isn't making me like him, for sure."

"Have you told Peter about this? He won't allow you to marry another man, Alivia. You two have been an item forever. Everyone knows this."

"I talked to Pete this evening. His answer was an emphatic no. The thing is, Morgan, that I feel God may require this from me. I've had a holy unction, as the pastor likes to put it, a nudge from the Holy Spirit."

"Why do you think that? Why would God ask you to give up your whole life because some man wants you? Don't make a quick decision based on emotion, Alivia. You should not allow another person, even your own father, to color your decisions."

"Jesus did, Morgan. He suffered much pain and agony for the good of His people."

"Alivia, you sound like you have lost your mind or something. Jesus was, is God. He gave up his life so that we could have eternal life with Him. You are not a god, Alivia."

Alivia picked up her pace as she stalked around her bedroom. "I am not a god. You are correct. I love my mother, Morgan, and am willing to do whatever it takes to keep her calm. The scriptures say, "Greater love hath no man than this, that a man lay down his life for his friends." I called you to ask you to pray with me about this decision. I'm between a rock and a hard place. My head says to keep Pete, but my heart says I should make the sacrifice for my mother."

"Wait. Wait a minute, Alivia. Won't your mother worry even more if you suddenly break up with Peter? I know for a fact that your mother and his mother have planned for this marriage since you were both in elementary school. Maybe even from birth."

"I know, Morgan. Dad seems to think that losing his company and our home will be too much stress for Mother. He wants to try his best to keep her relaxed. While this solution may help my mother to rest, it doesn't do a thing for my stress level."

"Are you saying that you will lose the ranch too?"

"Yes."

"Friend, you weren't kidding when you said you need prayer. I will absolutely help you pray about this decision. We will trust God, but at the same time, could we try to find another solution? Maybe your dad could offer to sell the company to him and get money."

With a deep sigh, Alivia answered, "He has already tried that, Morgan, and Mr. Travers's answer was an uncompromising no. No one is going to buy a company on the brink of disaster."

After the discussion with Morgan, Alivia was able to breathe. She ended the conversation and slipped into the bathroom to take a long soak in her favorite lavender bubble bath. She could do this. Maybe.

Chapter 5

The dark circles under Alivia's eyes confirmed that she had slept little. The problem went around and around in her brain and refused to let up. Did she have the strength to do as her dad asked? She imagined herself like a poor little hamster going nowhere, no matter how fast he ran on the wheel. What should she do?

She applied heavier makeup than she normally wore to camouflage the evidence of a restless night. Dressed in comfortable clothes, she headed downstairs to meet her dad before he left for work. She caught him as he was about to leave the house.

"Dad, wait up. I want to tell you that I am willing to discuss the situation you mentioned yesterday. I can't give you the answer you want right away. Frankly Dad, I don't know if I will ever have the nerve to do such a thing. There are so many factors, Dad. What about Pete? His feelings matter to me, Dad. What about his parents? Do you think they would remain friends if I should decide to marry someone other than Pete?"

He turned from the door to face her. "Sweetheart, I know I have asked a hard thing. If you decide that you positively can't do it, then I will have to accept your decision. You are not my first choice as a solution, believe me. I don't want to interrupt your life with my problems."

"Dad, have you prayed about this? Do you trust God enough to let the chips fall where they may? You have always said that

God's ways are higher than our ways, and that He is always working behind the scenes for our good."

He hung his head and said, "I have prayed, Alivia. It seems like God is ignoring me. So far, He hasn't sent me any relief. This situation is more difficult than anything I have ever faced. If I were the only one involved, I would just face the storm and do my best. When it comes to your mother, I can't stand by and watch her suffer. I made a vow to love and cherish her in sickness and in health."

Alivia took the time to wonder how her dad could stand by and watch *her* suffer for *his* mistakes. Wouldn't the vow cover all the family members? She held her tongue, but she had to clench her teeth to do it.

Opening the door to leave, he told her they would talk again when he got off work.

Alivia went to the kitchen in search of coffee. Black. Strong. Pulling a mug from the cabinet, she heard her mother enter the room.

"Good morning, Mom. What is that wonderful smell?"

"That's your favorite quiche I made this morning especially for you."

Alivia moved across the room for a long hug. "Mother, it is so good to hold you and to be held." What could be more satisfying than to wrap your arms around the person who gave life to you? The person who gave and gave of herself to others. The one who was always there to listen and to comfort.

"Punkin, I will never get enough of hugging you. I admit to you that I am glad school is over so that we may spend more time together. Now that you are back, I can confess how much I have missed you. Sometimes I would walk out to the stable and talk to Shadow and stroke her face and talk to her about you." She chuckled and said, "Shadow never said a word."

"Mom, if Shadow ever does talk to you, please run away as fast as you can." Alivia giggled as she pictured her horse and her mother having a conversation. "Mom, I have a week free before I have to report to my job. What would you like to do today? I'm game for anything."

"Hmm. I believe I would like for us to have lunch at the Creamery. We can stuff ourselves with their delicious food and then splurge on a chocolate sundae. Maybe a double chocolate, huh?"

Alivia laughed at her mother's funny face. "That sounds like a plan, Mom. I'm going for an early ride this morning as soon as I eat this delicious breakfast you prepared. Do you feel like coming with me? You do still ride, don't you?"

Not quite meeting her daughter's gaze she replied, "I rarely ride these days, punkin. I can't seem to get over the feeling of fatigue. Some days are better than others. Most of the time I feel fine as long as I don't do anything strenuous. I am certain that I can get back to my normal routine after the surgery in a few weeks. My cardiologist is very hopeful of my prognosis."

"OK, Mom. I'll see you in a couple of hours."

Alivia quickly turned from her mother to hide the tears that came unbidden to her eyes. It seemed her dad wasn't exaggerating about Mom's condition. She had never known her mother to take it easy before. After seeing for herself the weakness her mother exhibited, she could possibly understand her dad's concern. Maybe, just maybe, she would have the guts to do what her dad had asked of her.

Chapter 6

Alivia raced across the pasture but couldn't outrun her problems. Shadow was willing to go at whatever speed Alivia asked of her. She refused to allow her mindless worrying to spoil the day. She shook her hair free from the clip and allowed her honey gold hair to blow freely. For a short while, she would give herself permission to enjoy the morning.

Memories of her youth flooded her mind. Barrel racing. Rodeos. Competition. It was all a game that she loved. She loved the smell of the barn, the hay, and the oats mixed with the scent of horses—not *all* the scents from the horses.

Peter Miller's face was superimposed on every memory. It seemed they were almost conjoined twins. They grew up as close neighbors and enjoyed many excursions and vacations together as family. She couldn't remember a time when she and Peter weren't together, except for college. They chose different universities, much to the parents' dismay.

Of course, their wedding was in the family plans. If she decided to go through with Dad's scheme, would the families remain friends? Wouldn't it be just as hard on Mother to lose the lifetime friendship of Pete's family? Had Dad thought this through?

She had no answers as she and Shadow returned to her home. If God really wanted her to make this kind of sacrifice, He would have to show her the way. She had never even dreamed of doing anything so daring as her dad suggested. Her brain couldn't cope with the idea. How could her mind process something so bizarre and unexpected?

She had believed that her real life would begin as soon as she finished college. Her mind was geared to making plans for her future with Pete. It would take time to alter her pattern of thinking to encompass such foreign thoughts. This predicament wasn't in the forecast.

Calling out to her mother as she entered the house, Alivia put a smile on her face and tried to breathe life into her countenance.

"Mom, give me a few minutes to freshen up, and I'll be ready to go. I was thinking that maybe we could browse through that antique store that is close to the Creamery. I know you never tire of looking at old things that bring your grandmother to mind, especially some of those old dishes. You may even find another teapot to add to your collection."

Chuckling, Meagan answered, "I'll never forget the time you picked up a fragile teacup and the look of horror on your face when you dropped it. You thought the world had ended. You were about ten if I remember correctly. You didn't touch another thing for the rest of our shopping."

Smiling, Alivia added, "I remember. The scene is branded on my brain. It seems to me that you threatened me with certain punishment if I didn't stop picking up the items. Hmm?"

"Ha. Ha. You are right, punkin. You were accustomed to wheeling around on your horses and thought you should always be rowdy. Sorry, sugar, but you had to learn. Not every place is a rodeo."

Mother and daughter looked at each other and burst into laughter. "I was a little rough when I was young. I wanted to be a boy. I thought they had so much more fun than girls. I don't understand how you put up with all my shenanigans. It took a few years for me to realize that girls can have fun too."

Smiling at her daughter, Meagan replied, "Look at you now, punkin. All grown up and beautiful as well as intelligent. I always knew in my heart that you would be a splendid young woman with a heart full of compassion for others. You have exceeded my dreams, sweet girl."

"Now Mom, you're going to make me cry. How could I be anything but a nice person having you for a mother? We had best stop this or we both will be blubbering all over each other."

Chapter 7

Alivia awoke to sunshine and blue skies. She had told her mother that she would join her and her father in church this morning and hopped out of bed to get herself ready. She looked forward to the service. Pete had promised to meet her there with his family. After the service they would all eat lunch together, then she and Pete would spend some time together.

The praise and worship segments were special to Alivia today. Some of the youth participating in the music were kids that she had taught in Sunday school years ago. It seemed impossible that they were so old. Where did time go?

The pastor grabbed her attention when he announced a special visitor. A missionary from India was in the service and would speak for a few minutes. Alivia had a heart for missions and listened to every word the missionary said. Her heart stopped beating when he said, "You can give without loving, but you can't love without giving."

God, are you speaking to me?

She didn't hear another word after that statement. She had to force herself to listen to the pastor as he began his message. *What?* His sermon was all about being a servant. *OK, God. I get it. You are being very clear what you want from me. The question is, will I be able to do it? My heart feels like it is split right down the middle. I want to obey you, but I also want to continue with my plans.* She pulled out all the knowledge of the Bible and past sermons she had in her heart as she pondered the quagmire of her position.

Alivia shoved her doubts and tension aside as she left church with Pete. He was in a jubilant mood and whistled all the way to the car. "Alivia, do you realize that we haven't even started looking for an apartment or house? I want to find the perfect place for us. Do you want to use a realtor, or would you rather browse around on our own?"

Alivia drew in a deep breath before she answered. "I think we should wait a while longer before we look at houses."

"I know we won't lease anything yet, but I thought it would be fun to look. Somehow the idea of looking for housing makes the wedding seem nearer." With a huge grin plastered across his face he said, "You wouldn't be open to eloping, would you?"

She jerked her head around to stare at him. "No, Peter Miller. I would not."

Chuckling, he lifted her chin. "I don't want to elope, either. I just wanted to tease you a little. You seem too serious today. What's on your mind, Liv?"

"I have something to work out, Pete. I can't discuss it right now."

"Are you still fretting about your parents' problems? You already know how I feel about that. I'm sure your dad will figure something out, sweetheart."

"No. Yes. I'm so confused. No, I'm not confused, just unwilling to jump into anything. Pete, have you ever felt that God wanted you to do something, but you weren't sure you could do it? I mean, you were totally unequal to the task? We are supposed to live by faith. Do I have enough faith to take a leap into the unknown? I've always been prone to want a safety net, but this time there's not one available."

Peter placed his hands on each side of her face and spoke softly, "Honey, you are one of the most faithful people I know.

You are a strong Christian woman, and I think you are capable of great things."

"Even if it interrupts our plans, Pete?"

With a deep sigh, he answered, "You are talking about your parents, aren't you? Are you saying that you really do believe that God wants you to marry Dayne Travers? Why would he ask you to marry someone you don't know? Is the man a Christian? You know the Bible teaches against us marrying unbelievers. Besides, God wants us to be happy, doesn't he? How can you possibly be serious about this?"

"All I can say in answer to your questions, Pete, is that I don't know. Did you hear what the missionary said? 'You can give without loving, but you can't love without giving.' Those words slammed into me. Then the pastor preached about being a servant. What else am I supposed to think? God seemed pretty clear that I am to give myself to my family."

"Come on, Liv. God doesn't mean for you to sacrifice yourself and your whole future."

"How do you know this, Pete? What if he does mean it? He meant business when he told Abraham to sacrifice his only son, Isaac. I think I know a little of how Abraham felt. I believe God is asking me to give up my desires and dreams, or at least be willing to do so."

Peter ran his hand through his hair with a look of irritation. "Look, Liv, I love you and want to marry you. You say you love me too. If you love me, how could you even entertain the idea of marriage to someone else? Especially some stranger. We have known for years that we would marry one day. What am I supposed to do if you follow through with this insane idea? All my dreams and plans are wrapped up in you, Liv. Are you really willing to ruin my life?"

Alivia huffed out a reply. "Peter Miller, hold on just a minute. The plans were not *your* plans; they were *our* plans. The dreams were not *your* dreams but *our* dreams. Look at me. Take a good look into my eyes. Can't you see my pain, Pete? Can't you look at me and see the anguish I am suffering? You are not hurting all alone, Pete. I've never had to make such a difficult decision before in my entire life, nor one that had such serious consequences."

With pleading eyes Alivia said, "I've already explained the situation to you, Pete. I am asking you to give me a little time to get this worked out."

"No, Liv. I won't lose you now that we are so close to getting married. I have waited and longed for you too long. I want your commitment to me, Alivia. Please tell me that you will drop this idea at once."

Shaking her head she said, "Pete. I can't drop it. I must at least pursue this venture and see where it leads. I'm sorry, Pete. I really am." Tears ran down her cheeks as she looked at him, eyes begging him to understand.

Angrily, Pete answered. "Alivia, are you seriously telling me that you believe yourself to be on equal footing with Jesus Christ? He gave his life so that mankind could be reconciled with God. Do you actually think this sacrifice of your life is as effective and important?"

Alivia sucked in a deep breath of hurt before she answered. "Pete, you know I don't mean that. I'm only saying that Jesus gave his life in obedience to the father. I am willing to give up my plans and my will in obedience to the Father."

Pete put his arms around her and rubbed her back, speaking softly in her ear. "I'm sorry, sweetheart. I should not have spoken to you in anger and made you cry. Why don't we just put this subject aside for a couple of days and talk about it after we have both had time to think things through?"

Chapter 8

What was a girl to do? Her heart longed to do the right thing, but what was the right thing? The right thing for her would be to obey God. The right thing for Pete would be to continue with wedding plans, or would it? It seemed that each solution would be good for some, bad for others. She would ask her dad to pray with her about the decision.

She found her dad in his home office puttering around while his wife napped. He stopped and gave Alivia his full attention. "Sweetheart? Are you crying?"

"Yes. A little. I've been talking to Pete about our marriage, or should I say our possible marriage? Dad, I really need you to help me decide. My mind can't continue buzzing around the issue. I must decide one way or the other. This teeter-totter mind-set is killing me. Did you listen to the pastor and the visiting missionary this morning? It seemed that God was talking right to me. The whole service seemed to confirm what God wants from me."

"Honey, I've shared my thoughts with you about the situation. I hate for you to be so uncertain about this. Like you said, it seems that God has given you your orders. I will certainly pray with you and for you. God never calls us to do something without giving us the strength to see it through. He is all-knowing and sees your future as you cannot. He has a purpose for you, Alivia. I can't pretend that I know God's thoughts and plans for your future, but I do know God. It is always in our best interest to walk in obedience to him."

Pacing she asked, "Dad, do you think that God requires such real sacrifices from his people? I mean, how can I do this? Would I be a decent wife to Dayne if I'm forced to marry him? Would I forever hold it against him that I had to give up my fiancé for him?"

He rubbed his brow with a heavy hand as he lowered himself into the chair. "Maybe after you meet Dayne you can be a better judge. It is possible that you will truly like him. If you decide that you can't like him, we will call off the whole business."

"OK. Will you please be with me for the first meeting? You know I haven't been around many men. I was always hanging with Pete. I am almost nauseated just thinking about him."

Chuckling, her dad shook his head. "Alivia, you'll be fine. I don't know why you are so worried. You are as beautiful and smart as any young woman I know. Dayne is a fine-looking young man and is adept at conversation. He is accustomed to speaking with people of high rank and many foreign officials. Honey, do you remember when you started attending the private school? The first day you were sick to your stomach and begged to stay at home. I wouldn't allow you to do so. When you were picked up at the end of the day, you were excited to have made a new friend."

Smiling, she walked over to him and leaned into him with a hug. "Thanks, Dad. I do remember that day. Go ahead and call Dayne tomorrow and set up a meeting."

She left the room with a much lighter heart.

Chapter 9

Alivia received a call from Kenneth at ten o'clock the next morning. "Can you meet Dayne and me for lunch today?"

Biting her lower lip, she told him she could. "Where do I meet you?"

"Come to my office, and we'll go together. Dayne has a special place that he takes clients. We'll ride together from here."

For a split second Alivia played with the idea of making herself unattractive. Would Dayne Travers reconsider if she changed her looks? No, that wouldn't work. He had to have seen a picture of her at some point and would know she was masquerading. That could possibly anger him so that he would withdraw his offer to her dad. That thought brought up another one. Did Dayne have anger issues? Would he be abusive, either verbally or physically? How could she know for sure? Prayer and more prayer.

With nerves tied in knots, Alivia drove to her dad's office. She didn't ask him where they were going, nor did she care. She wouldn't be able to eat a bite wherever they went. As she followed her dad into the restaurant, breathing was all she could manage.

A tall man with jet-black hair approached them with a smile on his handsome face. Was this man Dayne? Her dad moved forward to give a handshake. OK, it seemed this was the man. Her breath literally caught in her throat at her first glimpse of him. She was not prepared for his looks, nor for his probing eyes that seemed to see through to her soul. What secrets were his eyes hoping to find?

Kenneth turned from the man to Alivia. "Dayne, may I present my daughter, Alivia. Sweetheart, this man is Dayne Travers."

In silence they eyed each other for several moments before Dayne broke the silence and asked them to follow him to a private dining room. A waiter seated them and gave each of them a menu. Alivia couldn't read a word. In a panic she said, "I'll just have a Caesar salad."

Dayne and Kenneth carried the conversation, talking about trivial matters. When the men had finished their meal and coffee was served, Kenneth turned to Alivia and said, "Alivia, dear, I think it's time for me to leave you two alone to get acquainted. He'll see that you get back to your car."

Alivia watched him as he left the room, then turned her attention to the man in front of her. "So, where do we start? I know your name is Dayne, and that's pretty much all I can say for sure. Would you please tell me a little about yourself? Wait. I would like to ask one question first."

With a frown on her lovely face she asked, "Why? Why me? There must be dozens of girls you could have at the blink of your eye. I truly don't mean to make you angry with me right off the bat, but why do you feel the necessity of buying a wife?"

Sighing, he began to speak. "Alivia, I do have a reason why I want you, but I can't share it with you at this time. May I just say that I have had a surfeit of pampered socialites and feel a need to move in a different direction. I am thirty-five years old, and I need and want a wife to share my life. Are you willing to give us a chance to see if we are compatible?"

"I am willing to try, or I wouldn't be here. But I must explain something to you. I am engaged to marry Peter Miller, and he is not OK with this arrangement. He is vehemently opposed to the idea, and he will try his best to block this attachment. I think you should know that my heart already belongs to Pete. Do you think you can cope with a wife who is in love with another man?"

"I understand. He wouldn't be much of a man if he didn't try to keep you. You have incredible beauty and a heart of gold to match." He failed to make any remark about her being in love with Peter.

"How can you know this when we have barely met?"

Dayne gave her a smile as he replied. "You are willing to give up your wants for the sake of your mother. Most people would not make such a sacrifice. Not one person that I know would even consider it."

Alivia licked her lips as she began to speak. "You have to know that I am considering this match because of your money. How do you feel about this?"

"Alivia, you are quite wrong. You are not marrying for money; you are marrying to save your mother from unnecessary stress. I love your dedication to family. It shows a depth of selflessness that is so rare as to be nonexistent. I want that level of caring in the woman who becomes my wife. Alivia, I have every intention of living with my wife for life. I don't like or believe in divorce except for drastic reasons. I have strong faith, and I want the same commitment from my wife.

"Please do not misunderstand me, Alivia. I want a real wife, not just a beautiful possession. I want to have children together to rear in a happy and faith-filled home."

Alivia pondered these words and made peace with her decision. "OK, Dayne. Let's begin our process of getting to know each other. My sister Natalie has twin boys who play baseball. They have a game at five o'clock this afternoon. Would you be willing to join me for the game?"

"Gladly. I used to love to play baseball. I would like to know your family also." As he drove her to get her car, they made plans for him to pick her up from home and attend the game.

Chapter 10

A livia was glad her mother wasn't around when Dayne knocked on the door. She would have had to give explanations that she was not ready to give.

She opened the door and almost went into shock. There Dayne stood before her. But not the Dayne from lunch. This Dayne was a cowboy from head to toe. He even wore a Stetson. How could the man look even more handsome than he had before?

Her heart gave a small lurch as she tried to think of something she could say that would prevent her lips from blurting out what she was thinking. Most of the time her thoughts were written on her face. Hopefully this time she cut them from her mind in time to keep from embarrassing them both. The man should be on the cover of every magazine in the country. How could a girl not gawk at him?

"Dayne, hello. Let me grab my purse and sunglasses, and I'll be ready to go."

As he opened the car door for her, she still had difficulty speaking. Good grief! Would she even be able to carry a conversation? No one had ever had this effect on her. Not that she had ever had much opportunity for feeling uncomfortable. Pete was her heart. She had never looked for or needed any other boyfriends. She had known from childhood that they belonged together.

For the twenty-minute drive to the ballpark, Dayne did most of the talking, asking about the boys and baseball. She was relieved when they arrived.

Natalie spotted them as they approached the small stadium and waved for them to come over and sit with her. She gave Alivia a questioning look as Alivia introduced her to Dayne. Alivia knew she would be in for a time of intense quizzing at the first opportunity.

"Dayne, come with me to the dugout and meet the boys. They will expect me to go to them."

The boys came tearing out of the dugout as soon as they spotted her, yelling, "Auntie, Auntie." She grabbed them up into a big hug and turned to Dayne. "These boys are my nephews, Parker and Peyton. Boys, say hello to my friend, Dayne."

Both boys instantly quieted as they looked him over. Finally, one of them ventured to say hello and the ice was broken.

Parker was first to speak. "Who are you, Mr. Dayne? Why are you here with Auntie?"

Peyton picked up the slack with his questions. "Do you have a kid playing ball too? Is he five years old like we are?"

Smiling at the boys, Dayne squatted down to their level and looked them both in the eyes. "I am here with your auntie, and no, I don't have any boys playing ball. I don't have any children at all."

"But we've never seen you with Auntie before. Where have you been? We've seen Pete lots of times. He said pretty soon we could call him Uncle Pete." Again, Peyton added to his brother's comments. "Are you going to be an uncle too?"

Dayne shrugged and said, "We'll see."

Alivia thought it was time to end the inquisition and suggested that the boys get back into the dugout. As they ran back to the team one of them yelled, "Bring us hotdogs with ketchup only. No chili, but lots of cheese."

"After the game. You are not allowed to eat in the dugout," Alivia answered.

"I'm sorry for all the questions, Dayne. They are curious about everything and anything and ask a million questions a day. And don't even ask them to walk anywhere. They always go at a dead run."

Dayne looked at her and smiled. "I think they are adorable. My brother has three children, and I spend time with them every chance I have. I am accustomed to being interrogated; believe me. I think that firing questions at people is a requirement for that age."

"That's a relief. I love those two little boogers as if they were my own. I really missed them when I was away at school. We FaceTimed often, which gave me a chance to keep up with their mischief. Parker is especially vocal and loves to tell me every little detail. Neither of them is completely still unless he is asleep."

"Ha. Ha. That sounds like my four-year-old nephew. I think he is all set to start T-ball soon. He'll expect me to be at the games. I love the interaction with them at this age. They are so cute in their uniforms and so proud of their accomplishments."

They found seats right in front of Natalie and her husband, who had arrived later. Alivia made introductions again. She couldn't stop herself from comparing the two men. Dayne with his jet-black hair and startling blue eyes beside Jonathan, with his sandy blond hair and cocoa brown eyes. They were similar in size, but Dayne seemed to have a broader chest and more muscles. Both were in the handsome department.

Alivia and Dayne joined her sister and brother-in-law in screaming their encouragement to the Eagles. Peyton struck out his first time at bat, but Parker made it to first base. None of the boys played like professionals and ended the game in a tie.

As the crowd cleared out, Dayne brought hotdogs to the bleachers and straddled a bench as he called the boys to him.

Something happened to Alivia's heart as she watched the connection of her sweet boys with Dayne. A softening she didn't expect. Oh no, she wouldn't succumb to his charms so easily and quickly. She pressed her lips together and hardened her heart.

Chapter 11

A livia persuaded Natalie to allow her to take the twins home with her. She had called her mother to make sure she felt OK for rowdy company. Alivia would have to take full responsibility for them. Did Alivia want the company, or was she trying to delay the conversation she knew was coming with her sister?

Dayne dropped them off but thought it best if he didn't come in with them. He made plans with Alivia for another date and left her at the door.

"Auntie, Auntie. Do you have another story ready? We've read all the books you gave us. No one writes stories as good as yours." Parker was all smiles. Certainly he knew he could influence Alivia with a sweet smile. He had it down to a science.

Laughing, Alivia agreed to a new story after bath time. "Please try to bathe without flooding the bathroom floor. If I must take time to mop the floor, I won't have as much time to spend with you two."

Two little heads nodded in agreement.

Alivia loved to cuddle them right after a bath when they still had the baby wash smell. Would she be allowed to spend time with them if she married Dayne? Would they ever get to spend the night with her? She thought of a hundred questions but had none of the answers. At least she could come up with a few questions for Dayne and contribute to the conversation.

The minute they were dry and had pajamas on, they jumped up on her bed and waited for her. They were all ears when she began the story.

"Once there were two frogs named Tootie and Tinker. They were best friends and wanted to spend every day together. One day Tootie's mom told him he had to come in and take a nap because Grandma and Grandpa would be there for dinner, and she wanted him to be rested for their visit. Naturally, Tootie didn't want to take a nap. He was too big!

"Tootie called Tinker and told him to meet him at the pond right after lunch. He planned to hop out the window so his mom wouldn't see him leave the house. He would play just a little while and then run back home and hop into bed. His mom would never know he had gone. About one minute after his mom had closed his bedroom door, he opened the window and hopped out.

"Tootie and Tinker had the best time ever! They hopped from one lily pad to the next, each one trying to jump farther than the other. They had a contest to see who could jump higher, who could hop faster, and who could be first to get to the other side of the pond."

Parker piped in with a question. "Did Tootie's mother catch him?"

"Not yet. They had so much fun, they almost forgot to keep up with the time. Tootie told Tinker they should race back home." Alivia smiled at the two boys and said, "These two frogs remind me of two little boys that I know.

"Tootie had barely made it back to bed when his mother opened the bedroom door and told him it was time to get up and get ready for their company. Poor Tootie was exhausted and wished for once in his life that he really could take a nap. He had to hurry and get cleaned up and put on fresh clothes.

"He was very glad to see his grandparents and hugged and kissed them several times before his mom called them all to come to dinner. When Tootie got to the table, he was so surprised! Mom had made every one of his favorite foods. There was horsefly casserole, toasted grasshopper legs, and dragonfly pie. Tootie loved the food but was so tired he couldn't keep his eyelids up. He fell asleep at the table, and his head dropped right into his plate! Grandpa laughed and laughed, then carried him to bed."

Peyton jumped into Alivia's lap and demanded another story. "Auntie, how do you make up all these stories? You should write them into books. I bet other kids would like them as much as we do."

"Thank you, sweetie. It's time for two tired little boys to go to sleep now. Hop on down to your room and get into bed. I'll leave my door open so you can call out if you need me."

Chapter 12

Alivia drove the boys home the next morning after breakfast. She was not exactly looking forward to facing her sister, but she couldn't avoid it forever.

Natalie met her at the door. After hugging the twins, she turned all her attention to Alivia. "OK, sister. Start talking. I want to know why you had some Greek god with you yesterday. It had better be good."

Alivia shrugged and looked anywhere but into Natalie's eyes. "Dad introduced me to him a couple of days ago."

"And . . . "

"Nat, I'm in a difficult situation. You know more than I do about Mom's heart condition. You've probably talked with her cardiologist, so you know firsthand how critical her problem is."

"Yes. I talked with him last week, and he told Dad and me that he didn't recommend waiting for the surgery she needs. What does Mom have to do with this guy?"

"Everything. Has Dad talked with you about his financial trouble?"

"What financial trouble?"

Alivia sighed. "So, he hasn't told you. I had hoped you already knew. It seems that Dad made some unwise financial decisions and has almost bankrupted the company. Because of her physical status, he cannot allow Mom to experience any stress at this time. He won't allow her to know about this business if possible."

"Alivia, you're making me crazy! Can you please talk faster? How does this tie into that man?"

Alivia did look her sister in the eye this time. "Nat, Dad has made a business arrangement with Dayne. Dayne will provide the necessary funds to get Dad's company back on track and will leave Dad in the position of CEO. There is a caveat; I must agree to marry him."

Natalie burst into laughter. "I'm sorry, Alivia, but this sounds so melodramatic that it can't be for real. This is your best story yet. I mean, who does that kind of thing nowadays?"

"Dayne Travers," Alivia replied.

"Sobering," Nat answered. "But Alivia, what about Pete? You can't just drop him after all these years of planning. He expects to marry you soon. Our families expect it. Have you discussed this with him?"

"Of course I have, Nat. Pete is one hundred percent against it. But what can I do? I can't watch our mother suffer needlessly when I have the means to stop it."

"Listen up, Alivia. You can't hurt Pete like that. It isn't right. There must be another way out of Dad's financial mess. You shouldn't give up all your plans. You don't know for sure that Mom isn't strong enough to make it through losing the company.

"We're talking about your whole life, Alivia, not some unimportant function. This decision would be majorly life altering for a lot of people. You must consider every aspect of this situation, Alivia. Both families would suffer unimaginable pain. It seems to me that a marriage to another man would compound the difficulties."

Alivia took a deep breath and answered, "Natalie, it isn't just the company. Dad will also lose the ranch and everything else we possess. It was all lumped together in the business deal he made. Dad feels sure that Mom can't handle the pressure of such a loss. You know how much she loves the place. It's hard to believe Dad made such an unwise decision."

"But Alivia, don't you think the stress surrounding your and Pete's breakup will be just as bad for her? What if the break causes friction for the whole family? Mom shouldn't have to be at odds with her best friend over this. Can't Dad work something out with the bankers?"

"He tried. I think Dad was relieved when Dayne met with him about taking over. But the stipulation worried him. I'm concerned about the tremendous load of stress that Dad is under. He could just as easily have a stroke or a heart attack. I can't stand idly by and watch my parents go through such a bad time when it's in my power to help."

Natalie shook her head back and forth. "Alivia, Jonathan and I could help him out, but I don't think we have the kind of funds that Dad needs."

"That's what I mean, Nat. It seems there is no other option. I will do this for them. I will spend as much time as possible with Dayne in the next couple of weeks. This will most definitely be speed dating."

"I'll pray for you, little sister. This is a difficult predicament to be in. Both you and Peter have a hard decision to make. I don't envy your position, but you have more gumption than I knew about. This will be a total act of selflessness. I'm not sure I could be as strong."

With a shrug of her shoulders Alivia said, "Hey. It can't be all bad. I mean, look at him. Killer looks and loads of money."

Chapter 13

Alivia and Dayne spent several hours a day together over the next week. She had finally gotten to the point where she could talk with him without almost throwing up. But she still had these little flips in her stomach when he was near. She was constantly aware of his presence. She and Pete had been so comfortable with each other that she didn't even have to think about how to act or worry about conversation.

Dayne had surprised her one evening when he brought tickets to the rodeo with him. She had viewed the event through fresh eyes as she sat beside him as a spectator and not a contender. This was one date when she felt comfortable enough with him to enjoy the action, yelling out encouragement to her favorite rider. Once when she jumped to her feet in excitement, she glanced at Dayne and noticed the smile on his face and in his eyes. It seemed that her exuberance did not embarrass him. What a relief she felt. She became a little less tense with him after that evening.

"Dayne, I think it's time for you to have dinner at my home and meet my mother. I have no idea what to tell her about you. I'm sure Dad hasn't talked much about you. Dayne, please tell me we are doing the right thing." Her eyes pled for understanding. They begged him for assurance that everything would be OK.

He put his finger under her chin and forced her to look at him. "Alivia, please trust me. Everything will work out." He placed the merest whisper of a kiss on her lips as she gazed up into his eyes. His beautiful eyes promised her he spoke truth.

She couldn't move. An invisible force tied her to him. What was happening to her? Did Dayne experience this magnetism? She had never felt this way with Pete. Should she have felt something more for Pete? She told Dayne to be at her home at six o'clock and had no recollection of what she did or said after that. She arrived at the ranch in a daze.

She found her mother at the end of the stairs. "Hi, punkin. You look a little flushed. You aren't coming down with a cold, are you?"

"No, Mom. I don't think so. Uh, Mom, I've invited someone for dinner tonight. I think you will like him."

Brows raised in question she asked, "Someone other than Peter?"

"Yes. It's someone connected with Dad's business. We've been out a few times."

"Does Pete know this?"

"Yes. He doesn't like it either."

"Sugar, do you know what you are doing? Are you telling me that you and Pete are apart now? I will not force you into anything, but you two have been together for years. Are you sure?"

Alivia replied honestly, "Dayne makes me feel things I never felt with Pete. My stomach flutters like I've swallowed butterflies. Is that normal, Mom?"

Meagan eyed her daughter closely. "Pete has never made you feel fluttery?"

She shook her head in denial. "I feel comfortable and safe with him. I'm beginning to wonder if Pete and I aren't better suited to be good friends. I'm not sure that Pete ever actually proposed to me or if our families just assumed we would one day marry.

"I'm falling hard for Dayne. I haven't known him long, but I feel a connection with him. Mom, when I am with him, I don't know where I am or who else is there. My eyes stay glued to his face. Oh dear. I sound like a teenager with a big crush."

Smiling, Meagan answered, "I love it, punkin. I want you to feel goose bumps run up and down your spine and think of your man all through the day. You'll need a strong connection and a stronger commitment to make it through life's trials. If you don't have that with Pete, then I want you to find it with someone else.

"Oh, I know Shirley and I have always dreamed of you two being married and tying our families together. You could have a good marriage with Pete. Dozens of couples started off as friends, but why settle for good when you can have amazing?" She got a faraway look in her eyes as if remembering her own courting days.

"Mom, I thought you would be upset. I've been so nervous to tell you that I've met someone special. I've worried that it would cause you more stress."

With a knowing look, she merely shook her head. "I don't remember one time that you came in from a date with Pete with your face flushed, unless you had been riding."

Dinner that evening seemed to rush by. Alivia was nervous that her mom wouldn't like Dayne, then afraid that she would. She wasn't completely convinced that she should drop Pete for Dayne. She knew she never would've thought of the idea had it not been forced on her. Was she so fickle that she could respond to anyone who paid attention to her?

She placated herself by admitting that it wasn't only looks. After all, Pete was a very handsome man also; but Pete didn't make every nerve in her body tingle in his presence.

When Dayne took her hand and led her away from the table, she thought she might faint. She was scared to be attracted to him. She had no fear with Pete. She blushed as she made eye contact with her mother. She walked with Dayne out to his car where they chatted for a few minutes. When he traced her jawline with his thumb and looked into her eyes, she was captured. Time stopped as he lowered his lips to hers in a tender kiss. He was not in a rush to end the kiss as Alivia surrendered to him. Was she dreaming? The gigantic Texas sky faded away as her world narrowed to Dayne.

Chapter 14

Alivia was up early and met her dad at the breakfast table. "Dad, I think I can agree with your plan. The only thing is, I feel like a horrible person. Do you think I am a shallow woman, Dad?"

"Of course not. You are a wonderful person, Alivia. Why would you doubt yourself?"

"I feel like I am cheating on Pete when I am drawn to Dayne. I talked with Mom, and she seems to be OK with our breakup. But Pete isn't okay. He is angry and very hurt. My decision will affect him more than anyone else. I hate to cause Pete any pain.

"I can't understand how I can be drawn to Dayne and be in love with another man. There seems to be a magnetic pull toward Dayne even though I try to resist. Could we possibly build a good marriage on our physical attraction alone?"

"Sweetheart, I don't believe that you have anything to worry about on that score. Dayne is already quite fond of you. I heard someone say once that if you act like you love someone, eventually you really will love that person. You are right to question this marriage if all you have for each other is a physical pull. Marriage is hard sometimes, honey, even for the most devoted couple. Have you and Dayne found that you are compatible? Have you discussed the serious issues that can tear a marriage apart? Money is a big trouble factor, but obviously it isn't going to bother you two. Another area you should agree on is children—yes or no? When? How many?"

Alivia stared at her dad. "Wow, Dad. You sound as though you are warning me not to make a hasty decision. Isn't there a need for speed?"

Kenneth reached across the table and placed his hand over hers in a loving gesture. "Sweet girl, yes, I am warning you to be vigilant and pay attention to any signs of conflict. It's much easier to solve a problem when it's just beginning. Always be honest with each other. Please don't allow a division to linger and become a stone wall."

"I'm listening, Dad. We have discussed topics that a couple would not normally deal with at this stage of our relationship. I feel confident that as we get to know each other better, we will get along well. Our marriage will be done in reverse, getting comfortable with each other after we are married. I'm not afraid, Dad. If it weren't for Pete, I know I would be excited about Dayne. He really is a very interesting and fun person. I find myself more and more drawn to him."

"Are you ready to plan a date for the wedding?"

"I guess so, but what will we tell Mom? She is a smart cookie, Dad, and we'll have to be extra careful how we word this decision so that she won't be suspicious and ask a lot of questions. Mom needs surgery soon, and I know for sure she would never miss my wedding. She told me the surgery is in three weeks. Do you think we should plan a wedding in two weeks? Will such a quick wedding distress her?"

Kenneth took both her hands in his and looked directly into her eyes. "Are you sure about this decision?" He gave her every chance to back out of the arrangement.

Alivia smiled and answered, "Yes, Dad. Let's do it. I would like for you to discuss this with Dayne, if you don't mind. I'm still just a little in awe of him. It is hard for me to believe he would go to such lengths to have me as his wife when he could have his pick from dozens of women. He has made it perfectly clear that he wants a real marriage, not a marriage of convenience." She turned and left the room.

Knowing how difficult the discussion would be, she took a deep breath and pulled out her phone. "Pete, can you meet me at the pond at the live oak tree? I'll be there in about fifteen minutes."

Alivia was wary of Pete's emotional state as she watched him riding toward her. He dismounted and went straight to her. "Alivia, you sounded pretty serious on the phone. Do you have bad news for me?"

She looked away briefly before she looked him in the eyes. "Pete, I have made the decision to marry Dayne."

"No, Alivia! You can't do this to us. I'm sure your parents' trouble will level out in time. If you follow the course you've set, we won't have a second chance. Please reconsider, Liv." His eyes implored.

Alivia had to turn from him to maintain control of her own emotions. "Pete, we've had this conversation many times. I feel in my heart that I am making the right move. I don't understand at all, but I do feel certain about my decision. I believe with all my heart that God is directing me."

He replied angrily, "How can you say that, Liv? What about us? What about me? We have planned for so long!" He turned her to face him and placed his hand behind her head and brought his lips to hers in desperation.

Alivia was amazed at the kiss. She didn't feel anything like she felt when Dayne kissed her. "Pete, I've made up my mind. I told Dad this morning to make the arrangements with Dayne."

With shoulders slumped in defeat, Pete walked back to his horse. With his vision blurred he turned around to face her one last time. "I can't stay around here and watch you marry another man. My firm has offered me a special assignment in Japan. I hadn't thought I'd take it, but now it seems like a lifesaver. I'll be gone at least six months. Goodbye, Alivia."

Alivia sat on the ground and allowed the tears to roll down her face and drip from her chin. She had said goodbye to her best friend in the world. A little piece of her heart broke off, and she felt the pain slice through her. She watched as Pete slumped over his horse and thought for a minute that he would fall off. She knew he was also feeling the heartrending pain.

Where was the joy of obedience? Shouldn't she feel comfort in knowing that she was obeying God? All she felt was the ache of broken dreams.

Chapter 15

The wedding was held in the botanical gardens in Fort Worth on a Saturday afternoon. It was a beautiful day for a marriage ceremony, with sunny skies and a myriad of flowers shouting their brilliant beauty. A slight breeze teased the petals to share their fragrance.

Alivia was beyond beautiful in the exquisite gown Dayne had purchased for her. She wore a veil that both her mother and grandmother had worn, a warm strand of pearls handed down from her grandmother, and a pale blue hankie stuffed into the bodice of her gown.

Only close friends and family attended the ceremony. Alivia breathed a sigh of relief when she saw Pete's parents. Morgan was her maid of honor, and Dayne's brother stood in as best man. Alivia was relieved when the ceremony came to an end. Staring into Dayne's eyes as he lifted her veil, Alivia emitted a soft sigh as his lips met hers. He whispered softly to her, "Everything will be alright. Trust me."

Alivia decided to believe him. With rosy cheeks and a big smile, she turned to face the crowd. Her heart sang a new song as she held tightly to his hand and greeted them. She went to her mother first. "Mom, I hardly know what to say."

"Your face speaks for you, punkin. I am so relieved you both decided on a short, I mean short, engagement. I so wanted to attend my sweet daughter's wedding, and I don't know how long it will take to recover from surgery. This was a perfect plan, and you both look absolutely stunning."

Kenneth butted in. "Come on, Meagan, don't try to hog the bride. I want a hug too." His eyes were teary as he hugged her close to him. "Sweetheart, I really do believe that you and Dayne will be good together. Thank you so much, Liv, for everything," he whispered.

Reaching out a hand to Dayne, Kenneth looked deeply into the young man's eyes and nodded. "Congratulations. Welcome to our family. We are honored to have you, son."

Acknowledging the older man's approval, Dayne replied, "The honor is mine, sir."

Parker and Peyton erupted through the crowd just as Alivia greeted Nelson and Sylvia Travers. "Auntie, Auntie. Is Mr. Dayne our uncle now? May we call him Uncle Dayne?"

Smiling, she answered, "Yes, you two. You may call him Uncle Dayne, but you interrupted our conversation with Dayne's parents. Do you think you should apologize?"

For about two seconds Parker and Peyton were subdued. They both shouted, "Sorry!" as they turned and galloped in the other direction.

"I'm so sorry, Mr. and Mrs. Travers."

Nelson and Sylvia exchanged a glance and burst into laughter. "Alivia, darling, you have nothing to be sorry about. We are quite accustomed to outbursts from our grandchildren. Before we had grandchildren of our own, I'm afraid we were quite critical of others whose children ran amok. Now we know the absolute adoration that grandparents feel for the children and allow them a little more leeway than we did our children." She laughed and said, "Both Steve and Dayne have complained about that fact."

Dayne recovered Alivia's hand and led her into the crowd to speak with his brother, Steve. "Brother, thanks for standing with me for the most important event in my life. I know it must have been quite a hassle rearranging your schedule on such short notice."

"I would have been angry if you had not allowed me to be best man. I am, you know, the best man." Steve smirked.

Dayne gave him a soft punch on the arm before he grabbed his hand for a handshake and then a hug. "Seriously, thank you. You are a great brother, Steve. You have guided me through some tough times. I appreciate you. Plus, you have made me an uncle."

"Dayne. You have jumped into this marriage rather quickly, but you two can make it if you keep your focus on the Lord. You remember Grandmother's favorite sermon. 'Seek ye first the kingdom of God, and all these things will be added unto you.'" They chuckled as they repeated the verse together.

Alivia smiled as she nodded in agreement. "My grandmother loved that verse too."

Having greeted each guest, Dayne decided it was time to escape with his new wife. He had planned a brief honeymoon, as Alivia needed to be close for her mother's surgery.

When the twins took time to notice that they were leaving, they ran to them. "Auntie where are you going?"

"I'm not sure, Parker. Dayne has made plans for us to fly somewhere in his plane."

"Don't do it, Auntie! Please don't do it!" he begged.

Bending down close to him Alivia asked, "Why not, sweetheart?"

With tears flowing he answered, "You will disappear if you fly away, Auntie, and we'll never get to see you again."

In shock, she questioned him. "Why do you think I will disappear?"

"Because. I've watched planes fly off before, and they got smaller and smaller until they disappeared. I don't want you to disappear. I love you."

"Darling, I love you too. You do not have to be afraid for me to fly. The plane gets smaller because it gets farther away, but it doesn't vanish. The plane will land at another airport, and then we will get back onto the plane and fly back home."

Alivia's explanation seemed to be enough, and he hugged her once more before he ran off to find his brother.

Alivia was calm as could be until she found herself alone with her husband. With hands spread across her abdomen, she prayed for her stomach to settle.

It seemed that Dayne could read her mind. He took her gently by the shoulders and brought her close to him. "Alivia, I couldn't catch my breath when I saw you walking toward me. You are so beautiful that I have no words to describe you. I can't believe that you are mine."

She reached up and traced his square chin, something she had been wanting to do since their first meeting. "Dayne, I've never . . . I mean we never . . . Pete and I didn't . . . I have no experience."

She looked up into his beautiful eyes and saw a gleam that she couldn't quite name. She kept her eyes on his until he lowered his head and pressed his lips to hers. Her eyes closed, and her thoughts froze in place as Dayne filled her mind and left no room for anyone else.

Chapter 16

Today was the day Alivia dreaded more than any other day in her years on earth. The day her mother would turn herself over to a cardiologist. Could the doctor possibly mend her mother's heart? Did he have the knowledge and expertise to do so? Mother had confidence in her doctor; Alivia wished that she shared that trust.

"Mother, I love you so much. You know we all will pray for you throughout the surgery. Dad, Nat, Jonathan, and Dayne are all here with me. I'm sure God will be with you."

"I'm in God's hands, punkin, just as I always have been." She smiled the special smile that she always shared with her daughter.

Alivia wanted to cling to her mother as the nurse came to wheel her down to the operating room. She refused to act like a baby in front of everyone, but she may have allowed herself to break down if she had been alone.

Natalie began a conversation by asking about Alivia's job. "What did you do about your new job, Alivia?"

"After discussing it with Dayne, we both decided that I should let the job go to someone else. I would have to take off for a month to care for Mom, and it isn't as though I will need the money from the job. We discussed a few things I might try out after Mom is healed. The boys have been begging me to write books. They say my stories are better than the other books they read. Also, there are a couple of charity organizations I'd like to join."

"What a great idea, Alivia. I know someone who I think will be interested in illustrating the stories. I have kept in touch with a girl I went to college with. She has a career in photography and freehand drawing. Her work is fabulous, and she will be easy to work with. Let me know when you are ready to start."

Dayne smiled in Alivia's direction as he helped himself to coffee. He lifted the cup as if to ask her if she wanted a cup. She nodded a yes and returned his smile.

The pastor from Greater Faith Church rushed into the room out of breath. "I apologize for being late. I can offer no excuse except to say traffic. Meagan is in good hands, I know. May I pray with and for the family?"

The other occupants of the waiting room were polite enough to give the family a moment of privacy.

Time crawled as they paced, talked, and drank too much coffee. Friends of the family stopped in and gave words of encouragement.

Alivia tried to swallow the lump in her throat as Shirley Miller stepped into the room. "Mrs. Miller. How nice of you to come by." While waiting to decide whether she should hug Shirley or not, Shirley solved the question by pulling Alivia into a tight hug.

Shirley glanced around the room until her eyes found Dayne. "Would it be OK if I stick around awhile? I won't if it makes you uncomfortable."

Dayne was the first to respond. "Don't feel that you must leave on my account Mrs. Miller. I think the more friends we have around us, the better we will be." The others voiced their agreement.

"You know that Meagan is my very best friend. I couldn't sit still at home when I knew she was having serious surgery. Alivia, I'm not angry with you. I'm sure that God will work everything for your good and for Pete's. I was gravely disappointed at first, but I have learned through the years that God works in his own way. He certainly has no obligation to explain every little thing to us. We must trust him to do what is best for us. There is usually a lesson or two involved in God's decision process, and like it or not, many times there is also pain."

With a tearful smile, Alivia drew her into another hug. "Thank you. It means a lot to me to hear you say this. I have really fretted about you and Mr. Miller as well as Pete. I still love you and your family. It cut me deeply to cause pain for you."

All conversation came to a halt when a nurse poked her head in the door and asked for the Rushton family. "If you will follow me please, Dr. Erwin wishes to speak with the family."

Dr. Erwin came right to the point. "Mrs. Rushton came through the surgery remarkably well. We had no trouble correcting the problem with the aortic valve. I don't anticipate any more difficulties, but one never knows with this type of surgery. We stopped her heart momentarily during the surgery, and she will slowly recover from the shock of this. We will keep her under close observation for the next forty-eight hours. Afterward, we can better determine her prognosis."

With thankful sighs, the family regrouped in the hall. Natalie spoke to Alivia, "Sis, I have to get back to the twins. Peyton is pretty sick with a sore throat, and they always want me if they feel ill."

"It's fine, Nat. I plan to stay at least for the first couple of visiting times." The sisters embraced and promised to keep in touch.

Dayne spoke up, "Why don't we all go to the cafeteria and have a little lunch. We'll have time to eat and get back up here for a visit when she leaves recovery. That always takes an hour or more."

Alivia was relieved that her dad kept a conversation going with Dayne. It gave her much needed time to collect her thoughts and time to watch her dad's interaction with Dayne. He seemed to really like and respect Dayne. It pleased her to witness their communication.

By the time they had finished their meal, they thought it possible that Meagan would be out of recovery.

Being able to see and touch her mother brought Alivia comfort. She insisted that her dad go home and get some rest while she stayed for the next visiting time. "Dad. You look ready to drop. Please go home and lie down for a while. You don't have to promise to nap, but it would ease my mind a lot if you would only go and rest. Please, Dad."

"Alright, sweetheart. I must admit that I got very little sleep last night. Knowing we had to face this surgery early this morning kept my mind buzzing all night."

Looking at Dayne she asked, "Is there something you need to do this afternoon?"

He crossed the room and took her hand. "The only thing I must do is be by your side."

Alivia smiled in relief. She would not have asked him to stay and was both surprised and pleased that he offered. There was no denying the benefits of the human touch. She didn't know at the time that she would come to rely on Dayne more and more as the days passed in a combination of hope and anxiety.

Alivia made it through the next several grueling hours as she waited impatiently to see her mother again. Meagan was awake but could not speak with the tube in her mouth. Alivia did not know she would still have the intubation tube they had used during surgery. Her nurse told Alivia she would have the tube for the next two to three days so the heart could rest.

The sights and smells of the hospital almost overwhelmed Alivia. She would be thrilled when her mother was released and could be at her home again. It didn't help Alivia's nerves any to pass by the other patients in the ICU and hear their moans and miseries—not to mention all the tubes and blood she glimpsed on her way out of the unit. Alivia felt gratitude for the nurses and was glad that other people could do the job, for she certainly couldn't.

She stood by and watched one family react to bad news. *God, please help this family cope with this horrible loss. And please, God, keep my mother safe and let her heal quickly.*

After the midnight visit, Kenneth went back home. Alivia assured him she would be there throughout the night and would call if there were any changes.

Dayne tried to get Alivia to go home too, but she was adamant about staying. He made himself as comfortable as possible in the small recliner and kicked back to keep his wife company. Alivia looked at him in wonder. "I can't believe you are willing to sit up with me tonight. I would be OK on my own."

"Tell me the truth, Alivia. Don't you feel just a bit more at ease with me here beside you?"

She looked him in the eye and gave an honest answer. "Yes."

"Enough said."

Chapter 17

Alivia followed the same pattern for the next two days. She allowed herself time to go home and shower and put on fresh clothes, then went straight back to the hospital.

At ten o'clock on the third night, Dayne insisted that she go home for the night. "Alivia, you are about to collapse from exhaustion. How will your collapse help your mother recover faster?"

She nodded her weary head in agreement.

"Ride with me, and we'll pick your car up tomorrow," Dayne suggested.

"No. I need my car. What if I were to get a call during the night?"

"Then I would drive you back up here."

Shaking her head she said, "Thank you, but I'd feel better if I have my own vehicle handy."

"Then I'll drive behind you to make sure you are safe. If I notice any wobbling in your driving, I will be forced to take action."

That remark earned him a small smile.

Everything went according to plan—until Alivia noticed her fuel light blinking. "Oh no. Really?" She had no choice but to pull off for gas. She looked in her rearview mirror and saw that Dayne was right behind her.

She observed nothing as she put the fuel handle into her gas tank. She locked it in place and leaned against the car. She was past tired and hoped the tank would fill quickly.

She was unaware of the people beside her and was shocked when suddenly a hand covered her mouth and roughly forced her into another vehicle. "Stop! What are you doing?" This protest earned her a box to the jaw. She slammed into the inside panel of the van and everything went black.

A car full of young teens had just left their car to go into the convenience store. They had noticed a pretty blond at the gas tank. When the old van pulled out, she was nowhere to be seen. One spoke and said, "I think that blond-haired girl has just been kidnapped. We'd better tell the store clerk to call the police."

"Are you crazy? We can't get mixed up in something like that. The cops will try to pin it on us."

"We have to. Just think how you would feel if this happened to your family."

The clerk eyed them with suspicion. "You expect me to believe that you just witnessed a kidnapping? Maybe you were in on it."

Angrily, one replied, "Don't judge us, man. If you don't want to call the cops, I'll call them on my cell." He jerked his phone out of his pocket and dialed 911.

The police were there in ten minutes. Naturally, each one of the teens was questioned. They expected no less. They told the officer that an old, white panel van was parked at the pump next to the girl, and when the van left, the girl was gone too.

"Did you see the men in the van? Can you give a physical description?"

"I only saw the driver. He was hefty, had a dark complexion, maybe Hispanic. His hair was black with a ponytail that came about midway his shoulders. I didn't get a look at the others, but there must have been at least one other person in the van.

It seems that someone else grabbed the lady while the driver went into the store."

"Were you able to view the woman? Did she seem alert to her surroundings? Did she speak to anyone?"

"We only got a glimpse of her as we pulled in. She was leaning on the car."

"Did you observe which direction the van went?"

"It took the south exit. That's all we saw."

After about forty minutes, Dayne pulled into the station to a lot teeming with police cars. He quickly left his car to get a better look. All color drained from his face when he saw Alivia's car at the pump.

"Officer, where is the woman who was driving this car? She's my wife. We got separated when a vehicle veered into mine, and we had to wait for police to come and process the accident."

"Do you have identification?"

Dayne pulled his license from his wallet and handed it to the policeman.

"Mr. Travers, it seems your wife has been kidnapped. Those boys may have witnessed the action."

Dayne snapped to attention and started toward the teens. "Sir, please do not approach them now. We have not completed questioning them. We don't want to chance compromising the crime scene."

Crime scene. Dayne couldn't believe those words were used in conjunction with Alivia. He should have been with her. Maybe he could have been able to stop such an occurrence. Why had he left her? He should have insisted she ride with him. He knew she was exhausted.

As he approached Alivia's car, the officer directed him once again to step back. He had never felt so helpless in his life. It seemed he would not be allowed to help his wife at all. Never had he been in the position of doing nothing. He had people he could call. He had managers and directors, security and investigators, lawyers and tax people, yet not one of them could be of service now.

God, I don't even know what happened or how it happened. I ask that you take care of Alivia and bring her safely home.

The detective approached Dayne with one last question. "Can you tell us specifically what your wife was wearing?"

"Yes. She was wearing black boots, denim jeans, a lavender silk blouse, and a denim jacket."

It was three o'clock in the morning before Dayne left his wife's car. The police impounded the car to check for possible clues. The boys were finally released, leaving their contact information with the police. Dayne could take nothing with him. Not even her purse. Not even her phone.

Chapter 18

Alivia slowly regained consciousness. As she became aware of being in a moving vehicle, she listened to determine where she was. She heard men talking but they made no sense. She cautiously lifted her aching head. Maybe she was having a bad dream.

No such luck. She seemed to be lying in the back of a van or moving truck. The vehicle reeked of stale cigarette, unwashed bodies, and other odors she couldn't identify. If she didn't already know she was in a vehicle, she would wonder if someone had tossed her into a dumpster. She tried her best to relax and conserve her energy for later. She had no idea how much time had elapsed since the man took her.

Where was Dayne? Did they have him too? Why hadn't she listened to her husband when he told her to ride with him? She wouldn't be in this fix if she had only listened to his advice.

At some point, Alivia was aware of the vehicle turning onto a rough road that seemed to be an old dirt road. They must have exited the interstate. Would that make it harder for the police to follow? Surely someone knew she had been abducted. But what if no one knew? Her family would never know what had happened to her. She would simply disappear. *Please God, don't let this happen to me.* What damage would the news do to her mother? She was already in a physically weakened state.

The vehicle stopped, and she heard the doors open and slam shut. She was alone for several minutes and thought they had forgotten her. But no. She heard the side panel slide, and someone grabbed her and hauled her out. Moonlight bathed the scene with gentle silhouettes of the clouds and of the line of trees surrounding the area. It would have been beautiful had the circumstances been different.

All Alivia knew for certain was that they were in a forested area. She spotted an old rundown shed at about the same time one of the men shoved the tattered door open and pushed her in.

The acrid smell of moldy leaves and decay assaulted her nostrils. She felt around in the dark to investigate her prison. It seemed she was held captive in an old toolshed of some kind. Hands carefully moving across the walls of the small space, she noticed rotten walls and rusty tools. Maybe she could use one of the tools to gain her freedom.

Alivia drifted off to sleep at some point. Fingers of sunlight stole into the old shed to awaken her. Moving cautiously, she checked out the cell in the light of day. It was about as she had imagined. She doubted any of the rusted tools would be of use in her escape. It was mostly old plows embedded in the earth— too big and bulky for her to use.

To her delight, she found a sizable hole in the back wall possibly large enough for her to fit through. She pulled an object over to hide it from her captors just in case—in case she had an opportunity to run.

She stood when one of the captors opened the door. He looked her over and rattled off something in Spanish that she couldn't understand. Another member of the gang walked over and added his thoughts. He held a newspaper in his hands and gestured wildly.

Alivia gasped as she got a glimpse of the paper. On the front page she found a picture of the gala she and Dayne had attended a few days ago to raise funds for the homeless. Her own picture smiled back at her.

"What are you going to do with me? Why have you taken me?"

No answer.

"Please. Tell me. Let me go home, and I'm sure my husband will pay whatever you ask. I must get back to the hospital. Please. My mother is in critical condition in the hospital. I must get back to her!"

Nothing.

A third member came to her and spoke in English. "So, Mrs. Travers, is it? You look exactly like you do in this picture. I hear your husband is a very rich man. How much do you think he is willing to pay to get you back?" His evil grin sickened her.

"I don't know. Just name an amount you will be satisfied with. He won't pay a dime if you hurt me." She spoke bravely but hid trembling hands behind her back.

"Do you think I could have a drink of water?"

With a sneer he said, "No water, ma'am." He shoved her back into the shabby abode.

Chapter 19

Dayne rubbed his gritty eyes and tried to focus. His head of security sat across the desk from him. "Martin, get all the information the police will give you and start from that point. I have already called Cannon Investigators and expect them to start immediately. There will be several men on our team, and I expect a quick resolution. Talk with those three teenagers again and see if they remember anything. I'm not sure if the detective has told the boys not to talk to anyone else. Just work with it."

His voice trembled as he made a most difficult phone call. "Kenneth, I'm afraid I have some bad news this morning. Alivia was kidnapped last night." He shook his head as he answered a question from Kenneth. "Sir, I don't know how it happened. I followed her to make sure she was safe, but another car sideswiped me and caused me to be separated from her. Yes sir, I am already working on the problem this morning and have my best security on board. The detective from the scene has allowed me some leeway. He gave permission for me to be included in all decisions regarding the search.

"Kenneth, I wasn't a stone's throw from her the whole time. I just couldn't get to her! I have been beating myself for hours. I feel so guilty that I allowed such a thing to happen to her."

God please forgive me for not taking better care of my wife.
Is that your job or mine?

Swallowing the last drop of coffee from his cup, he decided his first stop would be to Detective Morrison's office. He hoped to catch him in his office as he pulled into the police parking lot half an hour later.

Dayne heard the news playing on television as he entered the detective's office. The officer had posted a BOLO alert last night describing the vehicle. So far, no leads. The newscast flashed a recent picture of Alivia and asked for information from any available source.

Dayne was the first to speak as he entered the room. "Mr. Morrison—"

The detective threw up his hand. "Phil, please. We'll be spending a lot of time together by the time this case is wrapped."

"OK, Phil. Have you received any ransom demands? Do you think they will contact me personally? I have to admit that I know nothing about this kind of thing."

"I'm not sure. By all accounts this seems to have been an impulsive move and not one well planned. It could be that they recognized Mrs. Travers and made the decision to grab her on the spur of the moment."

"How would that be different from a scheduled and planned kidnapping?"

"For starters, your wife apparently stopped at the station for fuel. They could not have known she would be at that particular place. Second, they did not take her purse or her car. In my experience, most small-time criminals will take every advantage. Your wife's purse was not touched. She could have a wad of money in it, but they left it."

Dayne nodded in agreement. Just as he was about to speak, the phone rang on Phil's inside line. He watched as Phil nodded and stood.

"We have another piece of information. One of the teenagers remembered an old worn bumper sticker that read Cinco de

Mayo. Also, the brake light on the passenger side was broken. This information could prove to be crucial. Let's go."

Phil led Dayne down the hall and up one flight of stairs to the special conference room the detectives used for the more urgent investigations. Dayne was impressed when he saw the operation. His heart eased just a beat or two as he understood that Alivia's recovery was top priority. *God, please lead these men to Alivia.*

Chapter 20

Alivia lost track of time as she sat in the stifling heat of the small shed. In her thoughts she relived the past several days, seeing her mother on life support, seeing needles and tubes all around her. Had the family informed her mother of her abduction? She hoped they had not divulged this disturbing information to her. She didn't want to be responsible for any delay in her mother's recovery from surgery.

Before Alivia could complete her plan for escape, one of the kidnappers burst through the door. He held a pencil and paper and offered them to Alivia.

"Mrs. Travers, ma'am, I have a little job for you. I want you to write a note to your darling husband. Write exactly what I say. No more, no less. Oh, while I'm here, I'll relieve you of that diamond on your hand. Wow! That's a very beautiful piece. We should get plenty of money for it. Meanwhile, we'll be waiting for your husband to drop a bucket of money on us." His laugh echoed through the camp. How she longed to slap his dirty face!

Alivia contemplated refusing. For a second or two. She took the paper and wrote what he told her to write.

After she handed the paper back to him, he pulled out a roll of duct tape. Her eyes opened in alarm as he came straight at her. "Yes, pretty lady. I'm going to make sure you don't decide to leave us before we are done with you."

He laughed his way out after taping her mouth and her feet, and taping her hands behind her back. She was left alone with nothing but her thoughts for company.

Alivia clenched her teeth to keep from crying. She decided not to waste energy on a futile effort; instead, she plotted. *The moon should be bright again tonight.* She heard the men laughing and joking, and from the sound of things, drinking. At least one of them had left in the van, leaving the other two to guard her. With luck, they would drink themselves to sleep. She settled herself as much as she could to conserve her strength for the escape.

As soon as darkness wrapped the camp, Alivia began her struggle to rid herself of her boots. She could walk with her hands behind her, but she could do nothing with her feet bound. It took her an hour to loosen one boot and soon the other followed.

Listening carefully, she heard nothing but snoring. Apparently, she had gotten her wish. She limped over to the corner and shoved the implement out of the way and began to slowly push on the rotten boards until the hole was big enough for her to squeeze through.

Standing behind the shed, she looked around. Nothing was familiar. She didn't know which direction to go. Which way was the road? Would she go deeper into the woods and get lost? If she found the road, would the van come by and catch her? All questions. No answers.

God, I could really use your help right now. Please guide me which way to go.

She started walking and followed what seemed to be a narrow trail through the dense foliage. In sock feet, she felt every bump and tiny twig she stepped on. It seemed she walked for hours with no help in sight. Would she wander around in circles all night? Isn't that what people do when they are lost?

She stumbled over a hard clod of dirt and fell to her knees, bruising them on acorns and sharp splinters of broken limbs. Wearily, she got to her feet to plod onward. Briars grabbed for her clothing and scratched her face, but she determined in her heart she would not give up. For just a moment, she allowed herself to think of her dad. He used to tell her that her stubbornness would get her into trouble someday. Well, this day her determination may save her life. She had to get as far away from the criminals as possible before they realized she was gone. She must get back to the hospital and keep watch over her mother. She sensed an urgency in her spirit.

With sweat pouring down her face, her primary thought was water; what she would give for a glass of cool water.

Her mind began to play tricks on her. She imagined she saw her husband laughing with a grotesque grin on his face. He had planned this venture for her and cackled with delight. Was it really Dayne's fault she was in this predicament? Had he changed his mind about wanting her?

Tripping again, she slammed headlong onto the hardened path. Her head found a sharp rock to fall on, and this time she did not have the ability or strength to rise. She lay where she dropped.

Chapter 21

Dayne had lain on his bed for a couple of hours but had no remembrance of sleeping. He could not relax when his beautiful wife was still out there somewhere, maybe suffering, probably frightened. He also was still using the guilt whip on himself. *If only . . .*

Grabbing his phone, he called Phil. "Did the team have the time to view the video footage from the convenience store? Were there other cars around at the time Alivia was there?"

"Dayne, I am sorry to report to you that the video gave us little information. From the angle of the camera, it showed only the van until it drove away. The van totally blocked your wife's car. There was barely footage of her car pulling up to the pump.

"There was some video of the teenagers pulling into the lot. They drove in within about five minutes of your wife's car. There were no other vehicles within twenty minutes prior to the panel van.

"It seems the van was about ready to leave when Mrs. Travers pulled in. We did, however, get a quick rear glimpse of the driver getting into the van. The description matched what one of the boys told us. The cashier remembered taking a twenty from the driver prior to pumping the gas. As his cap was pulled down low, it shadowed his face, and the clerk didn't get a good look. He confirmed that the man was Hispanic."

Dayne answered, "Phil, I have men searching surveillance videos all along the interstate, but so far they haven't found anything worthwhile. Have your men viewed footage of the interstate cameras?"

"We are working on that as we speak, but there are miles and miles of pictures from these cameras. The team is scanning as quickly as possible and pause the video only when a white van appears. It could be a couple of days before we have searched through all of them."

Breathing deeply, Dayne dragged his fingers through his hair. "I am jumping in for a quick shower, and as soon as I am dressed, I will head back to your office. I would love it if you could see your way clear to interview my head of security. Maybe you can both put your heads together and come up with another idea. I must tell you, Phil, that I have never encountered anything that has stopped me in my tracks the way this kidnapping has. I am willing to give any amount of cash they ask for to get my wife back."

Dayne received a hesitant reply. "Dayne, I think I can imagine what you mean, but giving in to the demand of kidnappers rarely works to the family's benefit."

"I have to at least try, Phil. My wife and I are newlyweds. I can't lose her before we have even had a chance at life together. There are so many things I want for us. I want to give her the world."

As he stood under the hot spray in the shower, his thoughts centered on Alivia. How beautiful and special she was. How she had charmed and captivated his heart as no other had been able to do. He could not give her up. He wouldn't.

Chapter 22

Alivia awoke slowly. Where was she? She tried to sit up but was hampered by something. What was wrong with her lips? She couldn't seem to get her mouth opened. Her throat begged for water. She tried to think, blinking her eyes and shaking her head to clear her mind. Shaking her head did not clear her mind; it only caused severe pain to shoot through her temples.

Oh yeah, she was running from the men who had grabbed her. *How long ago was it?* She couldn't seem to remember. Could she muster enough strength to stand?

Her intuition told her to keep running, but her run had changed to a slow walk. Her feet were bruised and bleeding; her knees ached. Her arms were numb from being pinned behind her back. She had to find help, and soon. She didn't like to imagine dying all alone in the wilderness. She put one foot in front of the other and kept going. One step at a time. Sweat dripped into her eyes, but she could not wipe her face.

She heard voices. *Were they real?* Had she circled back to the camp of kidnappers? She had to take a chance. As the voices got louder, she walked a little faster. There seemed to be many voices. Was she hallucinating again? Was her mind playing little tricks on her?

She took one final step into a clearing where there seemed to be a dozen or so men. She stumbled to the ground in front of one of them. Looking up, she faced the biggest and blackest man she had ever seen. One look into his eyes settled her. His warm brown eyes emanated peace.

"I am known as Tank. I will not hurt you. I'll be as gentle as possible as I peel this tape from your mouth. Then I'll cut your hands free. Maybe when you've been released, you can tell us who you are and what has happened to you."

"Water. Please. Water."

"We have no water. All we have with us is beer."

"Anything wet." With trembling hands, she tried to take a few sips from the can Tank offered her. Most of it went to her clothes.

Tank held the can for her, then gently massaged her arms to get the blood flowing.

With a quivering voice she asked, "Could you please help me remove my jacket? I'm so hot."

Tank carefully slipped the jacket from her shoulders. As he did so, Alivia scrunched her face in pain. "I'm sorry to cause you discomfort. I'll be as gentle as possible. Ma'am, can you tell us what has happened to you? Who you are?"

Alivia looked at him in confusion. What did he want to know? She slowly shook her head.

"It seems obvious that you have been imprisoned. Do you remember who bound you or where you were?"

Without answering, Alivia leaned sideways and laid her head on the jacket she had just peeled off. Dried blood covered temple and brow. Her facial features were distorted from swelling and bruising. Her strength spent; all she desired was to lie still.

Tank and the other bikers discussed what should be done and how to do it. Most of them wanted to distance themselves from the problem. Tank could understand that reasoning, but he could not walk away from the woman. She needed help desperately and quickly.

Taking a deep breath Tank said, "Help me get her onto my bike, and we'll determine if she can hold onto me. I can't risk her falling off and causing further injuries."

Two of the men roused her and helped her walk to Tank. It didn't take a full minute to figure out she could not hold herself up. It would be nearly impossible to do, but he had to put her in front of him.

After making plans to meet his friends later, Tank nestled Alivia into his shoulder and tried to determine where to take her. Should he take her to the police station? It was crucial that she receive medical attention at once.

About ten miles back, the men had passed through a small town. He would go there first. He sped down the road as fast as possible while driving with one hand and holding the woman. Luckily, there wasn't much traffic. He soon saw a sign pointing to the local police department, where he lost no time in taking her.

As he entered the parking lot, a single officer emerged from his vehicle, a toothpick hanging from his lips. He glanced at them and walked toward them. "Who are you? What do you want?"

Tank slowly stood to his feet while holding Alivia in his arms. "I found her a few miles down the road. She is desperate for a doctor. Could you help us?"

The officer took a good look at both and said, "The hospital is that way. I suggest you head in that direction immediately before I arrest both of you for drunkenness. Are you the reason the woman looks to be in such a bad condition?"

Tank used extreme self-control to keep from rolling his eyes as he answered the officer. "Of course not. I don't even know who she is. Do you have any missing persons reports?"

"No, we don't, so why don't you leave now while you are able?"

Tank realized he would get no help from the policeman—just as he had imagined from the moment he had laid eyes on him. He swung his legs over the bike and drove in the direction the cop had indicated.

Tank saw the hospital sign and veered into the emergency room entrance. Leaving his bike, he quickly carried Alivia in. The employee who manned the reception area looked at him with suspicion.

Without fanfare Tank told her, "This woman needs attention at once. She is badly dehydrated and has other wounds also. I don't know what has happened to her. She is confused and can't answer questions."

"Sir, we must have some form of identification."

Glaring he answered, "I just told you she is not capable of answering your questions. Now please get her to a doctor right now. She may be critical."

"And I just told you we need identification. Where did you find her? Didn't she have a purse or something?" Looking at him again with suspicion, she asked, "Is this a case of domestic abuse?"

"No! Look lady, you are wasting time. I tell you she has to see a doctor!" Tank did not often raise his voice, but he did so if the occasion called for it. By this time, he was ready to inflict severe pain on someone if he couldn't get help soon.

"We have a new director, sir, and he has reprimanded us for admitting people who could not pay. Without insurance or cash, my hands are tied."

Relenting just a bit she told him, "There is a clinic about six blocks south that will take her. They are federally funded and set up for this type of patient."

In a fury, Tank swung around and sped back to his bike. He would not allow the woman to die while in his care. He had witnessed too much dying in the last couple of years and did not wish to observe another death.

He found the clinic, and they took her at once to triage. He couldn't just leave her. There was probably someone very worried about her; if only he knew who.

He hung around in the hall listening as the doctor and two nurses examined her. "This woman is severely dehydrated. I can't get a needle into the vein. We must get some fluid into her. Call a nurse from pediatric to come down."

Alivia's body began to shake as she went into shock. Her blood pressure plummeted, and the oxygen level was dangerously low.

"We are losing this woman! We must get her airlifted to Dallas General immediately. We'll do all we can to keep her alive until the helicopter arrives. We are not adequately trained to do what is necessary."

Tank stood leaning on the wall in the hall, eyes closed, silently praying for the nameless woman. *God, I've seen so much death! Please spare this young woman. I don't know her story, and I don't have to know anything about her to know that she needs a miracle. Please allow the needle to be inserted so that she can receive fluids.*

"Aha! Success!" The pediatric nurse was jubilant when the needle went into the collapsed vein. "At least it's a start. I believe we have just increased her chance for survival."

Chapter 23

For two days, the phone rang incessantly in the detective's office. So many people called in with tips. It took time to check out each lead, time they did not want to waste on useless information. He finally got a call from a woman saying that she had the van in sight.

Excitement gripped Phil as he and Dayne rushed to the area. The woman's grandson had taken a picture with her cell and showed the officer. Sure enough, there on the bumper was the decal and one brake light was broken.

The informant was an older lady. She explained that she could not talk on her phone while driving, so she had pulled into the mall parking lot to make the call. She was afraid to keep following the van. What if the man realized he was being followed and did something mean to her? It had been only ten minutes since she saw the van.

Phil sent out information to every officer within a twenty-mile radius. "The white panel van has been positively spotted on the George Bush Toll. I want everyone on alert. Please advise when you have the van in sight. Do not, I repeat, do not try to take the man alone. You will have immediate backup. We do not know if he is armed. Consider him armed and dangerous."

Within minutes, Phil received the information that the van was on the shoulder of the road with a flat tire at the corner of Main Street and High Ridge Avenue. By the time Phil and Dayne arrived, there were three patrol cars surrounding the van.

Phil grabbed the speaker and said, "Come out of the vehicle with your hands in the air. I repeat, come out of the vehicle."

A scrawny man with a long greasy ponytail emerged a couple of minutes later. "Put your hands behind your head."

Officers surrounded the man while one checked him for weapons and cuffed his hands behind his back. He refused to make eye contact with the officers.

Dayne had never desired anything in his life as much as he wanted to rush to the man and demand answers. He had promised Phil that he would not interfere, but it was all he could do to refrain. He stood in the background, fists clenched by his side, doing his best to remain calm when his nerves were shouting at him for physical release. He wondered how a man was to remain in control of himself under such dire circumstances. Raw nerves and unrestrained stress did not help Dayne's emotions to remain stable.

One officer entered the license plate for information while two others searched inside the van. "Phil, come look at this." He held a diamond earring and several strands of blond hair in his evidence bag. Phil motioned for Dayne to come and look. "Do you recognize the earring? We will have to match DNA to determine the hair."

Dayne gasped as he viewed the diamond. "Yes, this definitely belongs to Alivia. It is one of a pair that matches her engagement ring. I gave them to her as a wedding gift." He lost control and rushed to the man and would have physically attacked him if it had not been for the two officers who held him back. "Where is she? What have you done with my wife?"

The man lazily replied. "I don't know what you are talking about. I don't have any woman with me."

The first officer called to Phil again. "Sir, we have scraped dried blood from the side panel and have found this note on the front seat."

The note was addressed to the police chief. "I am in a safe place. Follow the directions strictly, and they will let me go unharmed."

Dayne snatched the note from Phil and finished reading it. "Leave five million dollars in the flowerpot on the outside of Ryan's Liquor Store on Carson Avenue. No police. You must be alone when you make the drop. Or else I will die." Signed simply, "Alivia."

Breathing heavily, Dayne rushed back to the driver of the van. "I ask you again, mister, where is my wife? You had better give me the answer I want, or so help me I will beat it out of you." Dayne's eyes blazed with fury.

For the first time since being cuffed, the man made eye contact. "I don't know anything. This van belongs to my friend."

Phil pulled Dayne away from the scene. "Dayne, you promised not to interfere. There are certain steps we must take; we must follow protocol, or we could be forced to release the only suspect we have."

Phil nodded to one of the officers. He then rattled off the Miranda rights to the suspect. "We are taking you to the station as a person of interest in a kidnapping case. You have been caught with the vehicle of suspicion in the alleged kidnapping of Mr. Travers's wife. It will be better for you if you cooperate with us now."

He sneered at the officer and dropped his head.

It took a few hours to confirm that the blood and hair samples did indeed match the DNA for Alivia Travers. The questioning of the suspect became more serious. The district attorney allowed some flexibility in making a deal with the suspect. They had to find Mrs. Travers.

After what seemed an eternity to Dayne, the guy finally decided to cooperate and agreed to lead the police to the hiding place. Dayne followed in his own vehicle. He planned to grab

Alivia at once and get her to safety. He would let the police deal with the other two kidnappers.

Chapter 24

Without flashing lights or sirens blaring, the policemen turned onto the dirt road that led to the hideaway. The other two suspects gave no resistance, as they were nearly drunk and unable to make a satisfactory effort to escape.

Once again, the suspects denied any knowledge of a missing woman. How could they not know anything about Alivia when there were so many clues that tied them to the crime? In the search for clues, the officers found Alivia's boots in an old abandoned shed. "Mr. Travers, do these boots belong to your wife?"

Dayne paled as he viewed the boots in question. What had they done to his wife? Where was she? If God ever had plans to answer one of his prayers, Dayne hoped he would choose this one. He was desperate to find Alivia. Guilt ate at him like cancer. He should have taken better care of her. He should have picked her up, placed her in his car, and refused her request to drive home.

A detailed search was made around the perimeter of the campsite. Behind the old shed they found a couple of footprints. The dead grass seemed to have been trampled, and there were broken branches on several bushes that could have been made by a person or an animal.

Phil made the call to bring out the search and rescue dogs. Those bloodhounds could follow the least scent and were almost always accurate.

"Dayne, I'm asking you to trust our guys to find your wife. Please allow us to do our job. The dogs should arrive within the hour. Meanwhile, my officers will take these two suspects to the station and process them."

Dayne nodded wearily. He was about to drop from exhaustion. Every new clue brought him more alarm. Would they find her in time to save her life? What was her condition? Was she alone and frightened? Was she lost in these woods? *God, please help us locate Alivia. Please.*

The hounds sniffed Alivia's boots and immediately circled around until they followed a path through the woods. After trailing about an hour, they began barking. They stopped when they found blood on the ground.

Dread built up in Dayne until he feared he would explode. Alivia was bleeding. *How badly? Was she still alive? Had the kidnappers stabbed her? Shot her?* Placing his palms against his temples, he gave himself a stern lecture. He must not allow his mind to stay on the negative possibilities but switch his thought pattern to the positive side. They would find her. She would be OK. He would hold her in his arms soon, and their life could continue as before.

The dogs were released again to continue the search. After about half an hour, they stopped and barked excitedly. When the men caught up, they found the dogs standing guard over a denim jacket.

The officers took way too much time snapping photos of the jacket on the ground. In his head, Dayne knew they were being efficient deputies, but his heart longed for them to speed up.

Tire tracks indicated that several motorcycles had been in the area recently. The hounds circled around but were unable to pick up Alivia's scent again. Apparently, she had been taken by one of the bikers.

One of the deputies did find a very small trail of oil that led out of the clearing and onto the road. With careful study, they were able to follow the trail into the small town of Marion.

They were unsure if this bike carried Mrs. Travers, but it was the only clue to follow. It could be possible that whoever owned this bike may have some information they could use to find Alivia.

Dayne's phone rang, and he wanted to ignore it. As he glanced at his screen, he recognized the number of his investigator. He punched the accept button. "Dayne here. What? Are you sure?" Dayne grabbed his phone to call Phil and give him the information he had just received.

"Phil, I just got a call from a man on my search team. He came across evidence of a man bringing an unidentified woman to the hospital in a small town about ninety miles from Dallas.

"A large black man brought in a white woman who was almost comatose. She had no identification, and the man claimed he didn't know who she was. The receptionist called a friend and was talking about the couple. She thought the woman had been beaten, and the man apparently was big enough to inflict damage.

"The town he mentioned is Marion. Isn't that where we are now?"

Excitement built as the search team found directions to the hospital. The woman working the desk in ER knew nothing about such an incident. "My records don't show any new person has been admitted today. I just came on for my shift about half an hour ago. Do you need me to call Loretta to come back in?"

"Absolutely. We are searching for a missing woman who was kidnapped three days ago. The trail has led us here."

Rubbing his brow as he paced, Dayne wondered why this hospital had turned the couple away. It seemed that basic human decency would have caused them to at least try to help her. He had long ago used up what patience he had and was ready for action. He felt combustible.

About a half hour passed before Loretta showed up. Dayne wanted to shake the woman senseless! What had the woman been thinking? He forced himself to step back and allow Phil to handle the questioning.

"Loretta? I must ask you a few questions about a couple who came in several hours ago. Someone confirmed that a black man brought a white woman who was almost unconscious into this ER."

He pulled out a photo of Alivia and showed it to Loretta. "Can you identify the woman in this picture?"

Loretta stared at the picture before looking up at Phil. "I'm not sure. Maybe. The woman who came in looked like she had been badly beaten. I'm fairly certain the hair color and length would be right, but the woman who came in looked nothing like this young woman."

"Can you tell us where they went when they left here?"

"I sent them to a walk-in clinic about six blocks from here. You could check with them."

Leaving an officer to obtain necessary information from Loretta should they need her further, Phil and Dayne left as quickly as possible to check the next lead.

Both Phil and Dayne rushed into the clinic at breakneck speed.

Chapter 25

Alivia tried to open her eyes, but they seemed to be glued shut. Her arms and legs seemed to be tied down. Where was she? What had happened to her? She vaguely remembered escaping from the old shed, but nothing was clear after that.

Had the kidnappers recaptured her? She was tired, so tired. She heard distant voices and had the sensation of movement. How was she moving when her legs were bound? She heard a loud whirring noise and in her fevered mind thought giant birds had grabbed her into their clutches. She tensed, ready for this nightmare to end.

Video clips played in her mind's eye. Her mother lying still in a hospital bed. Pumping gas. Men grabbing her. An old tattered shed. Duct tape. A black man? A motorcycle.

As she tried to relax deeper into oblivion, she was aware of someone pounding on her chest. Why would anyone do that to her? Why wouldn't they allow her to rest? Alivia had a strange sensation of floating above the area where four medical personnel surrounded a person on a stretcher. Wait. Did she see herself? Her mother came to her and kissed her on the cheek. "I must go, punkin. My time is over."

She tried to hold onto her mother. "I want to go with you." Her mother shook her head. "No, darling. You must stay. Breathe deeply and embrace all this new journey has for you." She lovingly patted Alivia's face and was gone.

Chapter 26

Dayne used extreme self-control and allowed Phil to ask the questions. He pulled out the photo of Alivia and showed the receptionist.

"Yes, that could be the woman who was here. I can't be sure because she was in terrible shape. The man who brought her in was arrested. You will probably be allowed to talk with him at the jailhouse."

Dayne asked Phil to go to the police department to question the suspect while he talked with the doctor. He didn't want to waste a minute, even when he wanted with every fiber of his being to get a good look at the man responsible for bringing Alivia to the clinic.

Phil entered the local police station and gained permission to question the suspect. There sat a very large black man, elbows on his knees, head in his hands. His eyes were closed.

Phil took the lead. "Excuse me." The man calmly looked up into the eyes of the detective.

"I need to ask you a few questions." With a nod, the man agreed.

"I'd like you to look at this picture, and tell me if you have seen this woman."

Tank scrutinized the photo, then shook his head. "I can't say for sure. The woman I brought in was half dead."

"Please tell us what you can about her. This woman was kidnapped a few days ago and our search has led us here. Please tell us how you came to have her with you. Sir, you are a person of interest in this case. I have to make you aware of your rights before you speak."

Tank nodded. "I was with some buddies in the woods about ten or so miles from here. We had stopped for a breather and were ready to get back on the road when a woman stumbled into our midst. Literally stumbled. She had duct tape on her mouth, and her hands were taped behind her back. When I removed the tape, she asked for water but had to settle for a few sips of beer."

Nodding, Phil asked, "Can you confirm what the woman was wearing?"

"Jeans, light-colored blouse, denim jacket. She asked me to help her take the jacket off because she was so hot. She had nothing on her feet but socks."

Phil nodded. "Did she tell you who she was, or what had happened to her?"

Tank shook his head. "She was confused and disoriented and couldn't tell us anything about herself or her situation. She looked completely wiped out. I'm sorry for you if that woman is the one you are searching for. I helped her as much as I could, but I don't know if it was enough to save her life."

Phil said, "This information matches what we found in the clearing. I'm going to find out what the clinic has done with her."

After gaining custody of the man, Phil took Tank with him for further questioning at the Dallas headquarters and rushed back to the clinic. He found Dayne still waiting to see the doctor who was tending a critical accident victim. "Ma'am, where is the woman in question now? Did you give her medical attention?"

"As I've already told the other gentleman, you will have to wait to talk with the attending physician. He'll be able to answer your questions."

More than a few minutes dragged by as Dayne and Phil waited impatiently for the doctor. After several minutes, a man in a
white coat came toward them. "I'm Dr. Alvin Simpson. I'm the
doctor on call this weekend. I understand you have knowledge
of the Jane Doe we treated today."

"Her name is Alivia Travers, my wife. May I please see her
now?"

Doctor Simpson shook his head. "I'm afraid you're too late
to see her . . . "

Dayne grabbed the desk for support as his brain acknowledged the words "too late."

"Sir, you misunderstand. I only meant too late to see her because she has been airlifted to Dallas General as Jane Doe. We
didn't have a clue as to her identity, but we managed to get her
stable enough to transport.

"Quite frankly Mr. Travers, we almost lost her. Our crew
worked for about forty minutes before she was stable enough
to move. She should arrive at Dallas General within thirty minutes or so."

Breath gushed from Dayne as he allowed himself the first
glimmer of hope. He could possibly get to Alivia within an hour
or so.

He turned back to Tank and offered a handshake. With an
unsteady voice, he thanked him. "You more than likely saved
Alivia's life with your quick actions. I don't know how I can
thank you enough." Tears eased from his eyes and ran down his
face. "May I ask your name?"

With a slight grin Tank answered, "Julius Caesar Thornton.
My friends call me Tank."

"Seriously? Julius Caesar?"

"What can I say? My mother is a history buff."

"Well, Julius, when this is over and the dust has settled, I'd
sure like to talk with you. I'd like to compensate you in some
way."

Tank shook his head. "That isn't necessary, sir. I believe in divine appointments. I was in the right place at the right time."

Phil shook his head as he looked at Tank once more. "I'm so sorry, Mr. Thornton, but I have to take you back to Dallas with me for processing. We must follow protocol. I believe your story, but we must stay within the law. You must be investigated before you can be released."

Chapter 27

Dayne had a police escort down the highway toward Dallas General. He didn't even bother to look and see how fast he was driving. Using his Bluetooth, he called Kenneth.

"Kenneth, this is Dayne. We have found Alivia. She has been transported to Dallas General and should be there in a matter of minutes. No sir, I have not seen her. She is in bad shape, Kenneth. The kidnappers are in custody currently, but they are not admitting anything. Of course, they will be prosecuted to the fullest. I'm sure Alivia will be able to identify them when she has recovered."

With a catch in his voice Dayne said, "Sir, we almost lost her. The doctor who treated her said they had to work hard to stabilize her for transportation. She was unable to tell them who she is or what had happened to her. I won't rest until I see for myself that she is OK. I am on my way to the hospital now. Would you meet me there? I know you have been worried to death about her.

"I can't tell you how sorry I am that you have to face this, Kenneth, so close to losing your wife. I can't imagine how you are coping with so much disaster at once. I am praying that Alivia will make a full recovery. Sir, we must allow her time to recuperate before telling her about Meagan. I don't even like to imagine how she will react to the news."

Dayne finished the trip in silence.

He rushed into the hospital and found Kenneth waiting for him in the lobby.

"I have found out where they have Alivia. She was brought in through the emergency room but has since been transferred to ICU on the third floor. We won't be allowed to see her yet, but they promised me it wouldn't be long before they had her settled." Words seemed to gush from Kenneth as though a dam had cracked, talking as they hurried to the elevators.

Dayne searched Kenneth's face as Kenneth searched his. Neither one spoke as they made their silent perusal. Both looked to be at the end of their endurance.

They waited quietly for someone to tell them when they could see Alivia, each lost in his own fear and misery. With tired bodies and worried minds, they were easy targets for fear to expose itself and almost consume them. Almost.

Why had God allowed such tragedy to happen to Alivia? She was the most giving person Dayne had ever met. She did not deserve such punishment. If anyone must suffer, it should be he. Why did he allow his wife to drive that night? He knew she was too tired and too emotional to be at the wheel. Why didn't he take her firmly by the hand and lead her to his car for the ride home? This whole situation was all his fault, and he allowed guilt to immobilize him, temporarily.

Dayne finally took control of the demon who terrorized him with "what-ifs" and "if only." God knew all things. He would make this situation right. Dayne dug deeply and found a ray of hope and a remnant of faith to carry him.

They waited for about forty minutes until a nurse came to them and quietly told them they could see Alivia for a few minutes. It would be impossible to say which of the men in Alivia's life responded with the most emotion as they viewed the pitiful young woman lying in bed.

Kenneth swayed and would have fallen had Dayne not been near.

He looked at Kenneth and said, "Go home, Kenneth. There is no point in both of us being here overnight. You should go home and rest and come back tomorrow. I know you must make further plans for your wife's funeral. Please, go home."

Dayne, emotions already high, gently touched Alivia's face as tears slipped down his face. "What have they done to you? My lovely wife. I would gladly transfer the suffering to myself if possible." His heart twisted within his chest as crushing pain filled his being.

With barely a whisper he said, "I love you, Alivia."

Chapter 28

Alivia regained consciousness and slowly lifted her swollen eyelids. She eyed her surroundings in confusion. Where was she? Where were the men who abducted her? Was it all a dream? She would have to figure this out later when she had the energy to do so. Once again, she surrendered to the darkness.

Poor Dayne, stretched out on a very uncomfortable recliner, was unaware that she had awakened and continued his sporadic sleep. Nightmares frequented his restless sleep with visions of Alivia lying cold and lifeless. He had heard her voice calling his name over and over, but he found her too late. She was gone, leaving only a remnant of disconnected thoughts in his head. How was he to continue his life knowing that it was his fault that she had died?

On and on his thoughts went in a vicious circle until finally he awoke and sat straight up, relieved to be out of the grasp of the nightmare. He forced his reluctant mind to center on memories of how Alivia had looked on their wedding day. She was a vision of beauty, a smile stretched across her radiant face. Alivia was everything pure, everything right in his world. She simply had to recover!

With this thought uppermost in his mind, he tiptoed into her room and stood in silence at the foot of her bed. Sounds and the medicinal odor of the hospital assaulted his senses and begged him to leave. No. He crept to the head of the bed and leaned over to whisper in her ear. "Alivia, sweetheart, you must wake. I'm so sorry for your condition. I promise I will make it up to you. I love you, Alivia. I need you. Your family needs you. Please come back to us."

He lifted her hand and placed a gentle kiss on the palm, holding onto her as he prayed a silent prayer for her recovery. With eyes closed, he again missed seeing her eyes open for brief moments.

* * * * *

Alivia found herself in a sweet dream where she was in her favorite place on the ranch, under the live oak at the pond where she had spent so much time as a young girl. Bright rays of sunlight filtered through the limbs and warmed her body.

She had a vague recognition of someone, a man, but she couldn't see him clearly. He spoke to her, but she couldn't understand what he said. Who was he? He was not Pete for sure. Then she heard Shadow speaking to her. *What? Horses don't talk.* She heard the man say, "I love you."

She tried her best to respond, but she couldn't get her lips to form the words. She tried to lift her arm to pet Shadow, but again, she couldn't make her arms respond.

Chapter 29

Dayne left the hospital with strict instructions to the staff to call him the instant there was any change in Alivia's condition. He must take a shower and get into clean clothes. His mind whirled with ideas and questions about his next step.

Having found his wife, he relinquished all control over the kidnapping situation to Phil to handle. He would stay in the loop, but no longer felt he should be in the middle of the investigation. His main concern was Alivia.

On impulse, he called his brother. "Steve, I need you, man. I'm a complete wreck! I've been at the hospital since late evening yesterday and have come home to clean up. Could you please pray for me? I need special strength today. The possibility of losing Alivia really brought home to me how much I love her."

"You love her? I didn't know, Dayne. She is very beautiful and seems like a sweet young woman, but love? Have you told her that you love her?"

"No. She would think I'm an idiot."

Steve chuckled. "Sorry to laugh at such a time, but Dayne, no woman thinks the guy is an idiot when he says he loves her."

"You don't understand, Steve. She thinks we just met a few weeks ago, when in reality I've loved her for two years. She obviously doesn't remember me. If I say those words to her now, she will think I am insincere."

"OK. I think I get you. Our entire family has been praying almost nonstop since she was taken. I will pray especially for you right now. God, we come to you now and ask for physical and emotional strength for my brother, Dayne. Give him a calm assurance in his heart and strength for his tired body. Please help him to trust you through this trial. Thank you, Lord. Amen."

Taking in a deep breath, Dayne replied, "Thanks, brother. I have a new peace to get me through the next couple of days. The specialist caring for Alivia told us that the next forty-eight hours will be crucial to her recovery. Using medical terminology that I don't understand at all, he explained in simple terms that sometimes brain cells cling to moisture when they are threatened with dehydration. If they retain too much, they will swell, causing damage to the brain. As it stands, he isn't sure that Alivia will recover completely."

"That is tough, Dayne, but God's power isn't limited. He created us, and he certainly has the wisdom and the power to heal us. Trust him, Dayne. Trust him."

Chapter 30

A livia became aware of her surroundings as she forced her eyes open. She couldn't tell yet what was real and what was a dream, but her body answered the question with pain and stiffness.

Slowly she eyed the room, with all the medical paraphernalia surrounding her. With a deep frown, she tried to remember why she was in a hospital. Why did her head hurt? Why were her limbs so heavy? She spied the bandages around both wrists and wondered. Had she been in a car wreck? She closed her eyes and made a promise to herself that she would think later.

Alivia heard a distant voice speaking calmly to her. It sounded like Dayne, but why was he so far away? Did he really say the words, "I love you"? She thought she felt something wet dropping on her cheek.

"I am so sorry for what you have had to endure. If I could take the pain, I would gladly trade places with you. I haven't slept for three days except for little snatches of time. How could I sleep when the love of my life was in danger?" The love of my life? Dayne didn't love her, but the voice sounded just like his.

She tried to absorb the words she heard. "I could not stand to lose you so soon after I finally got you in my life. I've loved you for so long and hoped that one day you could love me. I want to build a life with you, sweetheart. I want to have children with you. My heart is full of love and joy. Please come back to us, Alivia. My life has no meaning without you." Alivia felt warm comfort envelope her body, enabling her to go into a deep and healing sleep.

Chapter 31

Dayne felt refreshed as he drove back to the hospital. He had checked with Kenneth to see how he was coping and made plans to meet him. As he pulled into a parking spot, he looked up and said, "OK, God. The ball is in your court. I am willing to accept whatever your decision is."

He met his father-in-law in the front lobby and prepared to grab the next elevator. He was cautiously optimistic as they exited on the intensive care floor. "Kenneth, I believe Alivia will be restored. I just had prayer with my brother a few minutes ago and feel a peace I have not had."

With a heavy sigh Kenneth answered, "Son, I will admit to you that the combination of this awful situation with Alivia and Meagan's death, my spirits are at an all-time low. If you can have faith for both of us, I would appreciate it."

"I understand completely, sir. I had to call my brother for reinforcement this morning. We cannot carry heavy burdens alone. I believe the scripture that says two are better than one. When one is down, the other can pick him up, or something to that effect. I'm pretty sure that applies to us right now."

With a half-smile, Kenneth nodded his agreement.

Nearing Alivia's room, they became aware of quite a stir in the hallway. They rushed to the scene to see what was going on. They were stopped at the door. "Sir, I'm sorry, but no one will be allowed into the unit at this time. We have an emergency to handle and will let everyone know when they are allowed entrance."

With a quick look at each other, Kenneth and Dayne retraced their steps to the waiting room. Several nurses hurried into the room as more doctors arrived and began yelling out instructions.

With quiet agreement, the two men sat with heads bowed in silent prayer. Each hoped the emergency did not involve Alivia. Tension was thick for the next half hour as they waited for information. They were grateful when a nurse finally allowed the visitors into the unit and lost no time rushing to Alivia.

As they approached, they both noticed at once that her eyes were open. With huge smiles, they went to her.

Smiling his relief, Dayne picked up her hand and leaned over to talk to her, Kenneth waiting beside him. "Alivia, I'm so glad you are awake. I won't ask you how you feel; that is obvious. Both families have been praying for your recovery. I won't ask any questions about the last couple of days. We want you to have plenty of time to rest and heal." He bent and placed a soft kiss on her forehead. "I am so relieved to see you awake and responsive."

Kenneth could not stop the tears that slipped down his cheeks as he gazed at his daughter. "Alivia, you have given us quite a scare. I am so relieved to see you awake. Can you talk to us?"

With scratchy throat she answered, "I can speak, but not very loud. My throat feels raw. I can't believe how exhausted I am. I feel like I've been beaten with a club."

"As far as we know, no one beat you with a club," Dayne answered. "Please wait until you have recovered before you try to think about the situation you experienced. I can only imagine the trauma you faced. Please don't push yourself to remember. If you need something else to think about, why don't you just think about your husband? I hear he is a pretty good fellow."

His words pulled a small smile from Alivia. Dayne was satisfied with her response.

Kenneth took her hand and talked softly to her. "Sweetheart, we are not going to wear you out by forcing you to talk. I'll be back soon. I love you."

"I love you too, Dad."

With a quick nod to Dayne, he left his son-in-law alone with Alivia.

Dayne's eyes never moved from Alivia's face. Relief flooded his being as he thanked God for her. Emotion choked his voice as he tried to speak. He lifted her hand to his lips and gave it a feather light kiss. "Alivia. Alivia. I can't express how thankful I am to see you doing so much better. I feel like I've aged at least ten years in the last seventy-two hours."

She tried to smile as she answered, "That's OK. I feel like an old raggedy woman, so I guess we match."

"You are a beautiful raggedy woman. Get some rest now, and I'll see you in a few hours. If you need the slightest thing, please tell a nurse and she can call me. I have left my cell number with them. Anything, Alivia."

Chapter 32

With a light heart, Dayne decided to follow up with Phil. He had been content to leave the situation in Phil's capable hands until he knew more about Alivia's condition. Now that he felt safe to leave the hospital, he called Phil for an update.

"Phil, hello. This is Dayne Travers. If you have the time, may I stop by your office?"

"Anytime Dayne. We're working your case right now, so come on in."

Dayne lost no time getting to the police station. Phil and a couple more detectives were at a conference table surrounded by piles of paperwork. He gave a quick rap on the door and walked in.

"Hi, guys. I just left the hospital. It seems that my wife will be alright in a few days. I've been too tense and upset to even think about your investigation, but after this last visit I am elated with her improvement and am now ready to get back to this case. Have there been any new developments?"

Phil responded, "We have run a background on Julius Caesar Thornton, and as far as we can determine, he has been truthful with us. He has an honorable discharge from the Marines after two tours in Iran and Afghanistan. I spoke with his commanding officer, and he had nothing but high praise for him. They would have loved for him to reenlist. Apparently, he left for personal reasons.

"Our resources show that three years ago his wife divorced him, supposedly because of his lengthy deployments. He is a top-notch technician and served in special operations for the last two years. A good guy from all accounts. I'd say it was a lucky day when your wife stumbled into him. According to Sergeant Thornton, the group was about to leave the area within minutes of her arrival. Some had already left."

Dayne answered, "I prefer to give God the credit for her rescue. There were so many people praying for her safe return."

With a look of doubt Phil said, "Yes, I know. But I know plenty of others who didn't get rescued in time. There is a small percentage of hostages that make it home alive.

"I have investigated the police department of Marion. It seems that the admittance clerk at the hospital called the unit to inform them of a possible homicide. She told them the woman was severely beaten and described the man in detail. They arrested Julius as a person of interest in Mrs. Traver's kidnapping and possibly her death. He was held in jail until I took over the case.

"I'm so sorry, Dayne. The very man who rescued your wife was hassled by police officers. They must have heard the news of the abduction and decided to play hero. It is unconscionable that they were so slack in their duties. They should have been on the alert for your wife's appearance. It seems they did not deem the bulletin as important to them since Dallas is almost a hundred miles away. Their department is not exactly a prime example of how police officers should carry out their duties.

"We have questioned the three young men. It seems they are just what they said initially—normal teenage boys who happened to be at the station at the same time as your wife was nabbed."

Dayne raised his eyebrows. "Normal boys who *just happened* to be at the exact station at the exact time to be of help? Again, I choose to believe that once again God orchestrated events.

There is no telling how long it would have been before someone else noticed Alivia was missing.

"I get it, Phil. Really, I do. You see so much of the darkness and evil that you have become accustomed to bad endings. Have I told you the doctor said that a matter of half an hour would have meant death for Alivia? If Sergeant Thornton had not been in that exact location, my wife would have expired there on the spot.

"I'll admit to you that I was very afraid for Alivia. My faith was tested with this situation more than at any other time in my life. I am so thankful she was spared that I can never say 'thank you' enough times to all of you who were involved in her rescue. I intend to reward the boys and Sergeant Thornton. Would you work with my personal investigator to answer the question of what would be best for each of them?"

Phil answered with a smile. "I have already begun a file on the boys. Within a few days, I will know everything about them, down to what gum they prefer.

"As for the three kidnappers, they are penny-ante criminals who have walked through our office a few times. Mostly they have robbed businesses, especially convenience stores. That could be the reason they were at the store the night your wife was taken. Maybe they thought a quick ransom would pay them bigger bucks."

Dayne rearranged his face into a deep frown. "I have no intention of allowing these men to get off with a slap on the wrist. They almost caused my wife's death. I believe in mercy, but when it comes to my Alivia . . . " His voice choked up, and he couldn't complete the sentence.

Phil nodded. "I understand, sir. We have completed the sweep of the wooded area and have found many things that tie the three men to the scene. Their fingerprints are all over the place, and we have DNA matches for each of them. Your wife's boots, along with her ring and earring found inside the van they were driving puts them smack into the middle of this case.

"Dayne, I have no doubt that all three will be put away for a very long time. We have more than circumstantial evidence, but we would love to talk with your wife when the doctor thinks she can stand it. It would be great to have a positive ID from her."

Dayne nodded his agreement. "I'll let you know when her doctor agrees. My personal investigator uncovered information that I'm not sure you have discovered. It seems that a police officer on the force denied help to Julius and my wife before they tried the hospital. He was abrupt and lost no time telling them to leave before he arrested them. It seems my wife lost the contents of her stomach on the officer's shoes. He was not happy. I'm just glad that he did not arrest them."

Looking at Dayne with interest, Phil answered, "We do not have those facts, sir, but I will definitely look into it. Rest assured I will have the answers by the end of this day."

Chapter 33

Alivia woke with a clear head. She raised the bed a few more inches to sit up. For the first time, it occurred to her that she hadn't heard from her mother and had no knowledge of her progress after her heart surgery. Pressing the nurse call, she asked for someone to come to her room.

As the nurse approached Alivia's bed, Alivia asked her about Meagan Rushton. "Is my mother in this hospital? I haven't thought to ask my husband about her, but I am anxious to hear from her."

With a sudden change of countenance, the nurse answered. "I will check on that for you, Mrs. Travers." She then made a quick exit.

Puzzled, Alivia looked around for a phone so she could call Dayne, but there was no phone in her room. She pressed the nurse call again. This time when the nurse arrived, Alivia asked for a phone.

"There are no phones in the ICU. I can call your husband for you if you'd like. Maybe he can bring you a cell phone."

Alivia had a moment of panic. "Why am I in the ICU? Please call my husband and ask him to come as soon as he can."

"Yes ma'am." She seemed relieved to escape the room.

Alivia couldn't account for the nurse's obvious discomfort. Was her condition worse than she thought? Was she about to die?

By the time her doctor made his morning rounds, Alivia had worked herself into a state of agitation. She knew nothing about herself or her mother. She needed answers.

She immediately bombarded her doctor with questions as he entered her room.

"What is wrong with me? Why am I in this unit? Why can't I use a phone?"

"Please calm yourself, Mrs. Travers, and I'll explain everything. Phones are withheld in this unit for the benefit of the patients. We cannot allow constant distractions for the patients who need rest and quiet."

With trembling lips Alivia responded, "I can't remember most of the details of what happened to me. Could you please get my husband for me?"

"Of course, Mrs. Travers. I'll have someone call him immediately. Before I give orders for you to be moved into a regular room, I would like to get one more CT scan. If everything looks good, I'll allow you to be moved. Your vitals are acceptable, but you must remain calm in order to heal. We certainly don't want to face setbacks now that you have progressed. I believe you will be fine, Mrs. Travers, with several more days of rest."

Chapter 34

Dayne rushed down the hospital corridor, excited that Alivia had asked for him. He approached the bed at once and picked up her hand, smile in place.

"Alivia, I am relieved and happy that you are fully cognizant. Our families have been worried and have prayed continuously for your recovery. I can't express how grateful we are for the progress you have made."

"Dayne, please tell me. Is Mother in this same hospital? How is she?"

Dayne was filled with a sense of dread. He had known this moment would come, but he was hardly prepared for it. Hopefully he would not be responsible for a relapse.

"Alivia, sweetheart, I wish I could take this pain for you. I know of no other way to tell you about your mother other than to just say it. She did not make it, Alivia. She passed away soon after you were kidnapped. I'm so sorry, honey."

Alivia crumpled, head falling forward into her hands. Tears flowed as her body shook.

Dayne clenched his teeth in an effort to hold back his own tears. Gathering her close, he stroked her back and spoke softly into her ear.

"Why? Why, Dayne? Her cardiologist gave glowing reports to us. How could she die?"

With a soothing voice he answered, "I'm not sure what happened. Her doctor said something about an aneurism, but quite honestly, Alivia, I couldn't pay attention because I was too concerned about your disappearance to listen closely."

"Why would God do that, Dayne? Why would he take her from us? We need her. I need her. I don't know what to do now."

He pushed her away from him to look her in the face. "Alivia, for now you should concentrate on your own recovery. It will be difficult for you, I know. But know also that I will be with you every step of the way. Lean on me, sweetheart. I am strong."

She fell back against his chest and allowed him to hold her and comfort her while she sobbed and hiccupped herself to sleep. Dayne stretched out on the bed beside her, refusing to let her go.

Chapter 35

Two weeks had passed since Alivia was released from the hospital. Two weeks of questioning the events leading to this day. Her mind played tricks on her. At times, she would forget about the death of her mother and reach for her phone to call her. As she punched in a couple of numbers, she would then remember. She couldn't call her mother. Ever again.

Her body had recovered from the trauma she had experienced, but her spirit was crushed beneath a heavy load. Her will to fight had died also. What was the point?

Dayne tried to coax her to eat, but her stomach rebelled. He tried to tempt her into going out to ride Shadow. She needed sun and exercise. But no. She refused. She had fallen into a deep and dark pit where there was no light, and no energy to search for light.

Not knowing what to do, Dayne turned to Natalie for help. "Natalie, do you think you could find time to bring the twins to see Alivia? I am not ready to admit defeat, but I'm about to run out of ideas to pull Alivia from this abyss she has slipped into. She is totally apathetic to any suggestion I make."

Natalie agreed at once. "This afternoon when I pick the boys up from school, we will swing by to see her. She has always been responsive to those two. Dayne, I apologize for not showing up at the hospital. I knew if she asked about Mom, I would be unable to keep the truth from her. I didn't want to be the one to tell her. Can you forgive my selfishness?"

"Of course, Nat. Don't give it another thought. It was my job to let my wife know her mother had passed.

"I will admit to you, Nat, that I am more than a little concerned for Alivia now. I don't want to watch her succumb to depression, but I feel helpless to prevent it. I love her, Nat. I would do anything in this world for her. How can we help her?"

"We both will work with her, Dayne. I'm glad you love my sister. Have you told her that you love her?"

He hesitated before answering. "No, not really. I told her repeatedly when she was in a coma, but I've not told her since that time. I'm sure you know all the details of how we came to be married. I'm not proud of myself for taking advantage of a bad situation to attain Alivia as my wife, but I could not stand by and see her marry Pete. "

"Tell me something, brother. How did you ever convince Mother that you two should marry so quickly? I've been puzzled by this question. Mom knew that she and Pete planned to marry soon."

With a smile in his voice he replied, "Nat, dear, I simply told your mother what I have just told you. I love her with my whole heart. I promised to take good care of her and be a loving husband and father."

"OK, but how could you love her after knowing her such a short time?"

"I have loved her for two years. She doesn't remember meeting me, obviously, but we did meet at a fund-raiser. I fell in love with her the instant I saw her and wanted to have her for myself. She was not silly and conceited like the other girls. She seemed to be natural and loving to those around her. She has a generous and open heart, Nat."

Natalie nodded her agreement.

"I really hate to admit to anyone, even you, that for those two years, I had an investigator follow her and observe her actions. "

Shocked to the core, Natalie responded in anger. "Are you serious? You had a tail on her for two years? How could you do such a thing and then tell me you love her with all your heart?"

Dayne reacted calmly to her fury. "Natalie, I had to be sure that I wasn't chasing a phantom woman. I've been exposed to many over the years, and I wanted a real woman to be my wife. Your sister showed no attraction to money, nor did she seek the limelight. She has a goodness that runs deep, and I can't tell you how much I esteem her character. Not that I am perfect, but I want to have a wife and family with Christian values at the core of the marriage."

"OK, Dayne. I guess I can understand that. Alivia is a special person and should be treasured. It seems that you are willing to do that, so I'll let you off the hook." She punched him lightly on the arm and said with a smirk, "Just don't ever make me have to come after you."

Chapter 36

Parker and Peyton catapulted into the room and ran straight to Alivia where she was resting on the sofa. "Auntie! We have missed you so much! We begged and begged Mom to let us go see you in the hospital, but she said that little boys did not belong in a hospital room. Do you feel better now?"

Alivia gave the boys a half smile and hugged them tight. "I missed y'all too. Yes, I am feeling better now. I am really tired, though, and can't play with you today."

Their little faces fell in disappointment. "Aw, we want a new story. Are you sure you don't feel well enough?"

She nodded and hugged them again.

Natalie took charge and ordered the boys to go to the car where their dad waited. "I'll be home in a short while."

As soon as the room was clear, Natalie focused her attention on her sister. "Alivia, I am concerned about you. You should be back to normal by now. Are you getting any exercise at all?"

Alivia answered defensively. "I don't feel like exercising, Nat."

"Would you go to lunch with me? We haven't had any sister time in a while."

"I don't want anything to eat, Nat."

Natalie looked at Alivia and said, "You need to eat lunch. If you won't go out with me, then I'll just make you something here."

"No, Nat."

"Yes, Alivia. You are beginning to resemble a skeleton, girl. You must put on some weight or you will be ill. I'll look in the fridge and see what you have. I know your favorites."

Alivia closed her eyes in acquiescence. Maybe she could force herself to eat a couple of bites and satisfy her sister. She would eat quickly so Natalie would leave, and she could go back to bed.

She sat in the kitchen and watched her sister prepare lunch. Natalie talked while she worked. "Alivia, your hair looks pretty bad. How long has it been since you washed it?"

With a deep sigh Alivia answered, "I'm not sure, Nat. Does it even matter?"

"Of course it matters! You simply must take charge of yourself, Alivia. I know your emotions are all out of whack, but you must at least keep yourself clean and presentable."

"Why? I don't care what I look like."

"Oh Alivia, honey. I do realize the pain you have suffered, and I know how hard it was for you to lose Mom. I miss her desperately too. But you have a lot to be thankful for also. Your husband is worried to death about you. Could you at least try to please him?"

With a stubborn expression on her face Alivia answered, "Oh really, Nat? You know how I feel? I'm pretty sure you don't. I never even had a chance to tell Mom goodbye. You were at the hospital when she passed. You could experience the last hours of her life with her, while I was tied up somewhere and abused by evil men who only wanted money and cared nothing about how much terror or pain I suffered.

"As a matter of fact, sister dear, it all led back to who my husband is. If I had not been married to a rich man, I doubt they would have bothered me. So, the very person you want me to please is indirectly responsible for my condition. What about that, huh?"

Alivia turned and left the room, while Natalie watched in astonishment.

Chapter 37

Alivia stormed to her room, slammed the door, and fell across her bed in utter exhaustion. Why wouldn't people leave her alone? Did they feel what she felt? No. She was tired of the family and friends trying to help her. They couldn't help. Why couldn't they get that? Didn't they catch on when she refused their calls and visits? Would she be forced to leave her home to get any peace?

After a long nap, Alivia searched the house for the housekeeper. She told her to move all her clothing and other items to a guest room. Why would she care what the housekeeper thought? It was none of her business where she slept.

Alivia stood at the entrance to the foyer and into the main family room. How she hated the ostentatious display of wealth. In her opinion, the décor was way over the top. Money shouted at her from every direction. *Money—*how she loathed it!

Dayne had told her that his ex-fiancée had supervised the interior designer. As he had supposed that Selena would live there with him, he had allowed her complete authority.

Alivia had never met the girl, but she must be an idiot. Alivia couldn't feel comfortable in any room in the cavernous house. Nothing felt or looked familiar. The whole house reminded Alivia of a staged house on display. She wondered if she could walk on the luxurious carpets with her shoes on. She would not have been surprised to see velvet ropes across doorways to prevent entrance.

Alivia did take the time to realize that she was slightly exaggerating. She was probably the only person to hate the house. OK, maybe it wasn't the house at all, but what the house represented—money. Dayne had too much of it, and she was uncomfortable with wealth. She had grown up with plenty of money, but not to the extent that he had. She much preferred something cozier with a feeling of home.

She tried to picture children in this house. There were too many breakable objects lying around. She would go nuts trying to keep a toddler from destroying them or getting hurt.

Before she could retreat, the front doorbell rang. She opened the door, and there stood a smiling Pete.

"Pete. What are you doing here? I mean, it's good to see you."

He stepped into the room and grabbed her into a bear hug. "Alivia, it's great to see you. I apologize for stopping by unannounced, but I have only a few days before I must report back to Tokyo. I had to see you, Alivia."

He pulled back so he could look her in the eyes. "You look tired, Liv."

"Why, Pete, are you saying I don't look good?" She gave him a small smile.

"You know what I mean, Liv. Of course you will always be beautiful. Liv, I am so sorry for your loss and suffering. Mom kept me informed on events here at home. I could not believe what happened to you. I prayed for you and your family during the whole awful episode.

"Alivia, I have found someone. I mean someone special. Really special. Her name is Rose, and she makes my heart almost beat out of my chest when I am near her. When I first met her, I couldn't form a complete sentence in her presence. Lucky for me, I finally got over my nervousness.

"Alivia, I am so glad that fate stepped in and stopped our wedding. I love you, but as a very dear friend. I understand that now because of how I feel about Rose. I hope that you and

Dayne feel the same way about each other. Please tell me you do."

Alivia looked at Pete and saw an old and familiar friend. "Pete, I understand completely. When I first met Dayne, my hands sweated so badly I had to constantly wipe them on my skirt, and butterflies took up permanent residence in my stomach. I hope you and Rose will have a great life together. I have only good wishes for you."

"Thanks, Alivia. I couldn't be totally at peace unless you could tell me that you did not make a colossal mistake. Rose works for the same company, and we both are filing a request for a permanent transfer to Tokyo."

"That sounds wonderful, Pete. Give me a call when you come back to the States for a visit."

Alivia was subdued as she closed the door on her childhood friend. *She* should be the one excited about Pete's job. *She* should be the one telling everyone goodbye. She leaned on the door as uninvited tears slipped down her cheeks. She was happy for Pete. She was.

Chapter 38

Morgan decided she would not take no for the answer again, so she drove to Alivia's home and knocked on the door until Alivia opened the door.

Alivia stared at her for a moment before she invited her in. Was today designated for her friends to converge on her in masse? Was this attack planned?

"Alivia, I simply had to see you. I want to confirm for myself that you are OK. Girlfriend, you look awful."

"Thanks, Morgan. You are the second person this afternoon to tell me that."

"Really? Who was the other person?"

"Pete. He just left."

"I thought he was in Japan. Did his job in Tokyo play out?"

With a sigh, Alivia proceeded to explain. "He is home for a few days to get his job all set up to transfer permanently.

"He also wanted to make sure I am doing well in my marriage so that he won't feel any guilt about his new love. He was so excited, Morgan. He is head over heels in love with this girl named Rose. If for no other reason than his happiness, I made the right decision not to marry him.

"It's funny. I am the one who sacrificed everything, yet I am the one left holding an empty bag. I was so sure that I was in God's will. Go figure."

Morgan placed her hands onto Alivia's shoulders. "Alivia, please listen to me. Things did not turn out the way you expected them to. OK. Deal with it. The situation now does not confirm that you were disobedient to God. We can't see the whole picture. As God's Word says, 'We are looking through a glass darkly.'

"Hear me. We can't see what is happening in the spirit world, girl. God is still in control of the universe, and he still has you in the palm of his hand. Even if you think otherwise."

"But Morgan, I gave up my future so that Mom would live. And then God took her anyway. How is that fair?"

"Really? You are standing here telling me that God isn't fair? Have you read the book of Job? God had to have a real 'sit down and listen to me' conversation with Job. He asked Job, 'Where were you when I placed the stars in the sky? Where were you when I told the waters how far they could go?' Alivia, don't you dare hold onto anger against God. You are no match for him. He created you, and he will work all things to your good. Trust him. Besides, didn't you make the sacrifice because you knew God wanted you to? Didn't you obey without restrictions?"

She hung her head and whispered, "Yes."

"OK then. Allow God to work in you, and be receptive to the lessons he wants you to learn. Surrender your anger and hurt to him, and let him cleanse you from these anti-God thoughts. These negative thoughts come from the enemy of our soul, and you know he is nothing but a liar."

Alivia's head snapped up, and as she grabbed her friend in a hug, she acknowledged Morgan's advice.

"Thank you so much for coming. I think I feel better already."

"You're welcome. Now head upstairs and shower, and put on a pretty dress for your husband. He has been worried sick about you. He really is a hunk, you know."

Alivia gave a genuine smile to her friend. "Get out of here, girl."

Chapter 39

Dayne was undecided on what actions to take. Should he insist that his wife see a doctor for the depression she suffered? Would time heal her? His heart ached with a piercing pain every time he thought about what Alivia had endured.

Would this setback ruin their chances at a happy marriage? Should he let her go? The very idea of sending her away tied his insides into knots. There had to be another way to help her.

He experienced a delightful shock as he entered the house and found his wife dressed and with a smile on her face.

"Alivia. You look great. Did something happen today to cause this change in your mood?"

"Yes. Two things, or should I say, two people? Pete and Morgan both came to visit me today. Pete is happily in love with a girl named Rose. I can release any guilt I felt over ruining his life. Morgan came by and preached me a sermon about listening to the wrong voice."

With a smile Dayne responded, "Tell them both 'thank you' for me. I have prayed daily for your recovery. You have no idea how happy it makes me to see you smiling." He reached for her and held her close to his heart. *Thank you, God.*

"Would you like to hear news of your abductors?"

Startled, Alivia pulled away from him. "I don't think I'm ready to talk about that yet, Dayne. Could we wait on that?"

"Sweetheart, I am so sorry. I'm an idiot to bring that up now. Please forgive me. There are a million other things we can talk about. Such as, where would you like to eat dinner?"

With a playful smile she answered, "In our dining room. I asked Lena to cook some of your favorite foods. I confess to an ulterior motive. I hope the meal will soften you up so that you can find it in your heart to forgive me. I realize I have been a bear to live with these last weeks. I'm so sorry."

"Oh, Alivia. You have done nothing wrong. If you need to hear the words, I'll say them. I forgive you. My heart is full of joy that you are feeling good."

She wondered if he would still be joyful when he got ready to go to bed and found that she had moved her things to another room. Should she tell him now? No. She wouldn't ruin the whole evening. Did she want to change her mind about the arrangement? No. She still had some issues to work through. She admitted only to herself that she still held onto resentment that Dayne had purchased her. She had sold herself to help her mother, and she had paid a high price; a price that still wasn't high enough to keep her mother living.

She felt deep down that God should have honored her sacrifice. She would not speak of it again, but she couldn't seem to stop the thoughts from scrolling through her mind.

So much for her recovery.

Chapter 40

Several weeks passed and still Alivia slept apart from her husband. In her heart, she thought she may be intentionally punishing him for the past events. She did manage to keep up her appearance, and to anyone who did not know her intimately, she seemed fine. But the outside did not show the darkening of her soul as she surrendered herself to the negativity of her situation. It seemed that every day she slipped a little further into the black hole of depression.

The root of bitterness that she had allowed into her heart was growing rapidly, and she felt it was impossible to stop the growth. She fed and watered the seed as she continued to ponder the unfairness of her situation.

How could a loving God do this to her? He expected obedience, but then he left her high and dry when she did obey. What kind of God did that? Her mother should have lived. The sacrifice Alivia had made had been in vain. God knew ahead of time that he would take her mother, yet he had allowed her to go right ahead and marry Dayne, a stranger.

Around and around, Alivia's thoughts circled in her head until she thought she might go crazy. The same thoughts, the same feelings kept repeating over and over in her mind. She wanted to run away but knew she couldn't do that to her remaining family. Her dad grieved deeply over the death of his wife, and Alivia had compassion for him.

Should she give in to Dayne's suggestion that she see a doctor? What could a doctor do for her other than give her medication? No. She would not go see anyone. The fact was, she did not want anyone, even a psychiatrist, to see the extent of despair she had reached.

Nights were the worst time for Alivia. As she lay in her bed, she glanced up and saw a black cloud come into the room. In a panic, she turned her bedside lamp on. When she turned the lamp off again, she did not see the black spot, but she did not forget about it either.

After several nights of enduring the horrible nightmares, she finally got to the point where she screamed aloud. Dayne, heart thumping in fright, dashed into her room to see what had happened. He found Alivia sitting in bed, hands gripped in front of her chest, with the most abject look of misery on her face that he could hardly stand to see her. "Alivia, sweetheart, what is wrong? How can I help you? Do you feel like talking about it?" Giving her no time to answer, Dayne scooped her up and carried her to his bed. He held her close as he prayed softly over her.

The next morning, Natalie brought the twins over to spend some time with her in the hopes that they may prod Alivia into a better mood. Every time that Natalie had tried to talk with Alivia, she got the same answer. "I'm fine; stop worrying."

Parker was the first to reach her as he had been the first to exit the vehicle. "Auntie, I've missed you! Will you please come with us to the park? There is a whole new playground that we haven't been to yet. It has super tall slides and all kinds of stuff to play on. Please come."

Alivia grabbed him up into a tight hug and kissed his little cheek. "OK, little stinker, I will come. You have to promise me something, though."

"What? I can't say yes until I know what you want me to promise. Peyton neither. Does he have to promise too?"

"Absolutely. I want both of you to promise that you won't slide faster than I can, and you won't swing higher than I can. Is it a deal?"

"Deal." They both danced around her in excitement that she had finally said yes.

With a grin, Alivia looked at her sister. "Well, Nat. It seems that you have gotten your wish after all. The two monkeys have convinced me to leave my cocoon for the afternoon."

Natalie smiled in delight. "I'm so glad you have agreed to go with us, Alivia. The boys always have more fun when you are with them." She gave Alivia another quick look and said, "You will also benefit from this outing."

Alivia slowly nodded her agreement. "Nat, it's not as though I feel bad on purpose. I try; I really do. Sometimes I feel good, and I get a false sense of peace, and then here I go again into the pit. But for this afternoon at least, I think I can hold the demon at bay."

"Today is all we have, sister. We will take pleasure in today."

Chapter 41

Alivia paced as she waited for Dayne to get home. She had thought and thought until she felt ragged from the process. She couldn't foresee what Dayne's reaction would be to her idea. How could she when she barely knew him? Her heart grieved for the past—her mother, their home, her carefree life. If she could just go back home, she may be able to escape her prison of doubt and repressed anger.

Taking a deep breath, she met him at the door. "Dayne, I'm glad you are home."

Smiling, he answered. "I'm glad to be home too." He gave her a brief and gentle kiss on her lips. "How have you been today? Same question, but hopefully a different answer today."

She took both his hands in her own and pulled him into the family room and sat down with him. "I need to discuss something with you, Dayne." Still holding his hands, she looked into his beautiful eyes. "Dayne, I want to go home for a few days. To Dad's, I mean. I need to ground myself, and I don't think I can do that while living here. I don't feel at home here. I feel disconnected from all things familiar."

Dayne squeezed her hands but allowed her to continue speaking.

"I feel like a ship without an anchor. I can't seem to find my place, Dayne. I want to. I want to be carefree and happy again. I want to laugh and dance and enjoy life. But I feel like I am smothering. There is a dark cloud over me, and at times I'm afraid that it will consume me. Tell me what to do, Dayne."

He pulled her to her feet and wrapped his arms around her. "Alivia, honey, I'm not sure what to say to you. I want those things for you also. I wish I could make all the bad go away and wrap you in a bubble of contentment. I can't do that, Alivia. I can, however, allow you to go spend some time on the ranch. That is probably the best thing for you to do right now. Is there an aunt or other close family member that can give you counsel?"

She shook her head. "The only nonprofessional person that I can think of is Mrs. Miller. She is almost like a second mother to me. I can talk to her about anything. At least, I once was able to do so. I'm not sure how she feels about me now, though."

Dayne lifted her chin so that he could make eye contact. "Alivia, from all that I have learned about Mrs. Miller, she will still love you and would probably be pleased to guide you. I don't know much about counseling. I know that the body and the spirit are two entities, and that the body can feel pain even while the spirit soars. You are a strong Christian, Alivia. God will bring you out of this slump if you will allow him to do so. Are you sure I can't persuade you to see a professional counselor?"

Knowing it would disappoint her husband, she shook her head. "I do not feel comfortable airing all of my private thoughts to a stranger, Dayne. I'm sorry I can't be the person you want me to be."

"Alivia, never say that again. You are exactly the person I want. Now and for always. I chose you for several reasons, sweetheart." His heart was heavy with pain for his wife. What should he do? How could he help her? What if she left and never came back?

Tears ran down Alivia's cheeks at his tender care. "I'm sorry to hurt you, Dayne. I feel terrible about it. I haven't been able to think of an alternate plan instead of going to the ranch. I wish someone would tell me what is best for me and then force me to do it."

"Shhh." He wiped the tears with his thumbs and looked at her in her grief and almost went to his knees. He would do whatever was necessary to see her well again.

"Do you mind if I stay with you tonight, Dayne? I want to feel your arms around me again. I've missed you." She didn't even realize she was sending mixed signals to her confused husband. She did wonder if she could sleep without the usual nightmares with his arms around her giving her a feeling of safety.

"Honey, I'm thrilled to have you with me any time it's possible." He hoped with all his being that this would not be a final time. How could he endure a lifetime without her?

Chapter 42

A livia sighed deeply as she pulled into the driveway of her parents' home. Was she doing the right thing? What else could she do? She could not tolerate another day in the mausoleum Dayne called home. Should she discuss moving into a different house? No. There was nothing wrong with the house. The fault lay within herself.

After she unpacked her clothes and put them away, she quickly went to the stables to saddle Shadow. Shadow always calmed her. She was the one constant in Alivia's spiraling world.

Shadow usually spent most of the day in the pasture. As there were no stable hands about the place, Alivia went to the pasture and called for Shadow. She never came.

Alivia went back inside the stable and found Shadow in her stall. Shadow tossed her head and whinnied her welcome to Alivia. She pawed at the ground and seemed to have trouble breathing. Alivia quickly led her from the stall and began a slow walk outside.

What was wrong with Shadow? Her actions were unusual and alarmed Alivia. Where were the stable attendants? She called loudly for Joe, but no one came. Finally, she tethered Shadow and went back into the stable to Shadow's stall.

What she saw infuriated her! Her food trough had remnants of oats and pelleted food, her water pail was completely dry, and the stall was littered with filthy straw. Alivia didn't know what was going on, but she had every intention of finding out.

Her first phone call was to the vet, who promised to be there within the hour.

Next, she called her dad. Waiving the usual greeting, she got straight to the point. "Dad! What is going on over here at your place? I came out to ride Shadow and could not believe the condition of the stable."

He answered in a calm voice, "Alivia, I can't answer your questions. Have you talked with Joe?"

"It is pretty difficult to talk with someone who is not here. Please call him while I clean Shadow's stall and put fresh hay down. She will need to be contained when the vet comes. Please let me know what Joe has to say about these conditions." She hung up without further ado.

Alivia was on an adrenaline high and got the work done quickly, fuming with anger with every shovelful of nasty straw. She could think of no excuses for the neglect she saw in the stable. She intended to give Joe an earful when she saw him.

She was ready to receive the vet when he pulled into the grounds. Meeting him halfway, she began to explain the problem.

"It sounds like colic, but I can't be sure until I check her out. Tell me what you know."

In a huff, Alivia answered, "I found her stall in the worst mess I have ever seen. Too much grain in her food dish and not a drop of water. By the looks of her stall, she must have been left for at least two to three days. I am so mad!"

"What did Joe tell you?"

"Nothing. He isn't here. Dad agreed to call him, but I haven't heard from him yet."

Dr. Yeager was silent as he examined the sweet horse. "I don't like what I am hearing in the gut. She possibly has a blockage or a twist in the intestinal track. Her breathing sounds labored. I'd like to treat her for a couple of days as though she has colic. Sometimes a horse can release the gas buildup with exercise. Withhold the grain and allow her to eat grass and hay for a couple of days. Let me know at once if there are changes, and I'll come back out. Leave her in the pasture for most of the day and bring her back to her stall in the evening."

"Thank you. I'll do exactly what you tell me."

Alivia thought of many words she would use on Joe when she did get a chance to talk to him. For her beloved pet to be neglected was wrong. Just plain wrong! She would never leave the care of her pet to someone else ever again.

Chapter 43

Kenneth pulled into the driveway and was surprised when he saw that Alivia's car was still there. He thought she would have left hours ago.

Alivia met him at the door, still in a tizzy over Shadow. "Hi, Dad. Did you talk to Joe?"

"Hello, sweetheart. You are looking good today. Are you beginning to feel better? I have been worried sick about you."

Alivia gave him a tiny smile, one that never reached her eyes. "Dad, I am trying. But my concern right now is Shadow. What did Joe have to say about the neglect in the stables?"

"Joe is out of town. His wife said he received an urgent call from his mother three days ago, and he had to rush to the hospital to check on his dad. He had been in an accident, and the doctors were not sure he would survive.

"I did question Joe's wife about the neglect, and she said Joe had turned everything over to his assistant. The young man has worked with Joe for the last five years, and Joe thought he could handle the job. The thing is, this man was overcome with acute appendicitis. I guess that in all the confusion, he forgot about our animals."

Alivia huffed out her answer, "Animals are important too, Dad. I'll bet the man thought of his own family during the crisis. The only horse who was left in her stall was Shadow. All the others were in the pasture. I'll go back out and get them to their stalls and give them fresh water and food.

"Shadow is sick, Dad. She may have colic, but Dr. Yeager couldn't be certain. I left her in the pasture rolling around on the ground. I'm scared, Dad. I don't think I can survive another loss."

Her dad pulled her close to him and embraced her. "Sweetheart, horses don't usually die from colic. I'm sure that in a couple of days she'll be fine. Now, do you want to tell me the real reason you are here?"

With an expression of surprise, Alivia looked up at her dad. "How do you know I have another reason to be here?"

Kenneth chuckled and scraped his fist along her chin. "Alivia, you know you can't hide anything from me. After all, I have known you for over twenty-five years."

She hung her head. "You are right, Dad. I want to stay here for a few days to see if it helps me to refocus. I just can't seem to get my head straight. I don't know what to do, Dad. I don't know how to feel, or how to act, nor how to express myself. I feel like a kite flying around in the clouds without a string attached. Does this make sense to you?"

"Yes, Alivia, it does. At times I still feel overwhelmed a little myself. It doesn't seem possible that Meagan is really gone. It seems that she should greet me at the door as she did for so many years. I miss her terribly, sweetheart. But we have to remember one thing; we will see her again. Oh, I know it isn't the same, but it does give us hope knowing that she lives with Jesus, and we will join her one day. Christians have that hope, daughter."

"I know, Dad. But I want her now. I never even got to tell her goodbye! I should have at least been able to tell her I loved her one more time. I feel cheated, Dad. I want to look once more at her beautiful face and put my hands on her face. I want and need her advice. She was my anchor, and now I am floundering."

Kenneth lifted his daughter's chin and forced her to look him in the eyes. "Alivia, your mother was not your anchor. Jesus is. You must seek him for answers and for fulfillment. No person can guide you as he can."

"Like you did, Dad? Were you following his guidance when you made the agreement with Dayne?" Alivia put her hand over her mouth. She could not believe the words that had just passed her lips.

"Sugar, I have thought about that over and over. I still can say that I felt the guidance of the Holy Spirit. I am sure of it. I know it seems crazy, given the fact that Meagan died. But we can never see or understand how or when God is at work. We must trust him, Alivia."

"Yeah. I've heard that many times. I felt that God led me in my decision to marry Dayne. But was it really God leading me? I sacrificed everything I had, Dad. I gave up my future with Pete and laid aside my own desires and aspirations. From my point of view, I gave but I have not received. It seems all the giving was on my part."

"Does this make you angry at God, Alivia?"

She pressed her lips together before she answered the question. "I think I am a little angry with God, Dad. And maybe at Dayne too. Why couldn't he have loaned the money to you without the stipulation? It seems so archaic and self-serving."

"I am not at liberty to answer for him, Sugar. He had his reasons.

"Alivia? Didn't you tell me that Pete had found a woman that he is crazy in love with? What if you two had married as planned, and then he met this other woman? How would that have played out? Honey, you must trust that God has the best of plans for you. You are his, and he is yours. His ways are always right.

"I'll admit to you that I did kind of let go of my trust when I tried to do things in my own power to prevent Meagan from harm. Please don't follow my path, honey. Follow Jesus."

Chapter 44

Dayne was at loose ends. He couldn't concentrate on business. He couldn't focus on the financial reports in front of him. His mind was continually distracted with thoughts of his wife. What could he do for her? How could he help her? Would she be able to reason things out at her old home? Would she ever come back to him?

Questions by the dozen, but not one answer.

He picked up his phone and called his brother. "Steve, are you busy? I won't keep you but a minute. Man, I need some advice. You've been married for several years and should be able to shed a little light on my situation. Alivia has gone back to her dad's place. She said for a few days, but I am so afraid that she won't come back to me."

Steve smiled as he answered his brother. "I have one question, brother. Did you follow the last advice I gave you? You know, when I told you to confess your love to your wife?"

Dayne paused before he answered the question. "No, Steve, I have not told her that I love her. There has never been the right moment. I feel that she would not take me seriously if I were to tell her that now. Are there any other words of wisdom that you can share?"

"Call Natalie, Dayne. Get a woman's perspective. I'm sure she can help you. I know my own wife after all these years, but I surely can't understand other women."

"Steve, that sounds like a really good idea. Thanks."

Natalie did not answer her phone. Dayne left a message asking her to please call him as soon as possible. He turned his attention back to the reports in front of him.

About an hour later, Natalie called. "What's up brother-in-law? You aren't in the habit of calling me."

"I am desperate for your help, Nat. Alivia has been gone for two weeks. She said she needed a few days to get her head straight about all that has happened. Do you think she will eventually come back? I hate to admit it, but I don't really know my wife that well. We never got a chance to learn about each other before that awful kidnapping."

"Have you talked with her at all since she left?"

"Briefly. She doesn't want to be bothered, Nat. I think depression has a strong hold on her. I have suggested more than once that she should see a counselor, but she refuses."

"I have one idea that may work, Dayne. Court her."

"What?"

"Court her. You know, as in going on dates, sending flowers and all that stuff that men usually do when trying to win a girl's heart. You never gave her a chance to get to know and like you before you married her. I'm pretty sure she felt like she had no choice in the matter. Girls like to feel cherished and desired. We want to be gently persuaded, not snatched up."

"Wow. You know how to hurt a guy, Nat. I suppose you are right, though. I did rush her. I guess I can see that she would think me callous and egotistical."

"Ha! Two of my favorite words. You are too handsome, sweet, and have too much money. How could you not have an ego the size of Texas? No woman has ever turned you down that I can think of. Oh, wait. There was Selena. But she doesn't even count. She was not smart enough to know what a great guy you are. I'm so glad you did not marry her."

"Ditto! Do you think Alivia and I have a chance, Natalie?"

"Of course, you have a chance, Dayne. I would be honest with you if I thought otherwise. Alivia is a great girl, Dayne. She is a little gun-shy. Pete is pretty much the only guy she has dated. The other boys knew they didn't stand a chance if he was around. Right now, Pete is the one she uses as a measure for every other man. They have been great friends for a long time. It's going to take a little while, Dayne. You must use patience and perseverance."

"Thank you, Natalie. I will follow your advice. It can't hurt, and just maybe it will help. Before we hang up, I have one more thing to discuss with you. Has Alivia talked with you about the bad dreams she is having almost every night?"

Startled by the question, Natalie answered, "No Dayne. She hasn't even hinted at having nightmares. What has she told you about them?"

"She hasn't said one word to me. I know about them because I hear her in distress. Several times I've had to wake her up before she could pull out of the dream. The first time it happened she screamed out and almost gave me a heart attack. I thought that someone had broken into the house or something.

"She refuses to discuss the dreams with me, so I am not sure if she is reliving the kidnapping or if something else is bothering her. I'm worried about her, Nat. I am simply at a loss as to how I can help her. You do realize that she is temporarily staying at your dad's place, don't you? I had to let her go, Nat. I must allow her to process these disturbing events she has been through. I only hope that she doesn't decide to make the move permanent."

Natalie replied, "Dayne, I wish I could reassure you, but I can't get into her head now. I have no idea what is tormenting her other than the hurt of not saying a final farewell to Mom."

Chapter 45

Alivia had spent the whole afternoon with Shadow at her favorite spot on the ranch. The sunrays sliced through her cold heart and gave her a measure of warmth. There was a tiny hint of autumn in the air. She could tell that her tree was getting ready to shake the leaves from her limbs and would once again have bare, ugly branches.

She wondered what stage she would be in if she were a tree. Would her branches be full of green leaves? Would she be loaded with the beauty of yellows, oranges, and reds of autumn? Or was she in the winter stage of brown and ugly, with no beauty to be found anywhere on the tree?

Her thoughts were morose as she gazed into the spectacular sunset. God had given his people an abundance of color to brighten their days. Why couldn't she respond to the beauty that surrounded her? Why did her heart dwell on the barren nothingness of her life? She didn't expect answers, and she received none.

She mounted Shadow and returned home. As she neared the stable, she could see a bit of activity, unusual for this time of day. Had something happened to one of the horses? There was an unidentified truck and trailer backed up to the stable. She nudged Shadow into a faster pace and raced the remaining distance.

Two strangers were unloading a horse from the trailer. Why? Did they have the wrong address? Dad had mentioned nothing about buying another horse.

She leapt from Shadow and ran over to the men. "What is going on? Why are you unloading a horse at our place? We have not purchased one."

Their attention remained on the job at hand. One of them took the time to nod in the direction of the house. "Talk to him."

Alivia ran into the vicinity of the house and ran smack into Dayne. "Dayne? I didn't know you were coming today. How long have you been here? I have been out most of the day. Why are you here?

Dayne's entire face smiled at her. "I have a little surprise for you, Alivia. I hope you like it. Come with me, please."

He proceeded to lead her back to the stable and right up to the horse that was now out of the trailer and checking out his new environment.

"This is Sir Lancelot. I bought him for you, Alivia. I hope you like him."

She looked at her husband in confusion. Why? She already had Shadow and didn't need or want another horse. Was he using his money again, trying to buy her back to him? She shook her head and answered him, "He is magnificent! How could I not like him? But Dayne, I already have a horse I love dearly."

"Actually, Alivia, I bought him for a dual purpose. I thought that I would come out here every couple of days and ride with you. Do you have any objections to this plan?"

"No." She turned to him with a little bit of sass and said, "Am I permitted to ride him?"

He laughed at her cute face. "Of course. He is a gift to you, Alivia. Ride him whenever you want. If you prefer to ride him on our outings, I will use another horse."

Dayne was pleased with his first effort at winning his wife. He couldn't wait to try many other ideas. This would be fun. He felt a new sparkle in his world. Maybe Natalie was right. Maybe he could win Alivia through courting. What an old-fashioned word, but it fit Alivia perfectly.

Chapter 46

Dayne stayed for dinner and spoke mostly to her dad during the meal. After dinner, Kenneth excused himself and left Alivia alone with her husband.

"Alivia, I hope you don't mind my dropping in unannounced. I told you I would give you time, and I will. Would it be OK with you if we sit and talk awhile? I would really like for us to become acquainted. I will not pressure you in any way. If you feel that I am pushing, please tell me and I will back off."

"I . . . I don't know how to answer you, Dayne. I think I would prefer to know in advance when you are coming. There are days that I feel like I must hide myself from life. I don't want to leave my bed. I don't want to even try to deal with issues." She did not divulge to him the frequency of the nightmares, nor the fact that she now always slept with a light on. Only light would keep the dark spot away. She admitted it to herself. She was afraid. Very afraid.

"I am trying my best to understand you, Alivia. I can see that you prefer to isolate yourself from all unpleasantness. At some point, though, you will have to face these issues head-on. I promise you; I will be with you through it all. Please allow me into your life, Alivia."

"We are married, Dayne. I can't exactly take myself completely out of your life. I think I would like the chance to get to know you better. I agree to your plan."

Dayne wanted to jump up and give someone a high five. *Thank you, Lord.*

"Tell me about your rodeo days, Alivia. I know that you once competed in the barrel racing. Did you do other competition?"

Alivia smiled a real smile at him. "I did try the steer roping once. After many tosses, I finally got the lasso around the steer's neck and jumped off my horse to tie the feet together. The only thing was, the steer weighed more than I did, and I never got the thing on the ground, let alone tie his feet together. I think I came in dead last on that event."

Dayne could not stop himself from laughing at the imagery in his head. She had probably been a lot of fun to be with when she was younger, before she became loaded with pain and anxiety.

"Your turn, mister. I know somewhere in your life you must have faced embarrassment."

"Umm . . . I was quarterback, member of the Junior Honor Society, valedictorian, and aced my college entry exam. I have a special talent for numbers and have been successful in my businesses; however, I went to a birthday party once at the skating rink and couldn't stay off the floor! All my friends were dumbfounded. I was always good at any sport, and they couldn't believe that I could not skate. But I couldn't skate a lick. I was somewhat surprised too."

"Wow. I was beginning to think that I was in the presence of a perfect man. I'm so glad to realize that there may be some things you can't do well."

"I didn't seem to do too well with the girls. I never knew if they liked me or if they liked the spotlight. Basically, I guess I had a problem with trust. I've hit a snag a couple of times, which reinforced my lack of faith in the female species."

"Yeah. I can see that. You never did explain to me why you wanted me for a wife. How did you know you could trust me?"

"That story is for another day, sweetie. In due time I will tell you all about it."

Chapter 47

Alivia woke up with her mother on her mind. Perhaps the time had come to visit the grave. She would call Pete's mother and test the waters. She didn't feel that she could go alone.

She dialed the number to the Millers' home phone. Alivia timidly identified herself to Mrs. Miller. "Mrs. Miller? Hi, this is Alivia. I'm so sorry to bother you. I don't even know if you want to hear from me or not."

"Oh, honey. Of course I want to hear from you. I feel no ill will toward you. I love you. Is there something I can do for you?"

"Yes ma'am, there is. Do you think you can go with me to visit Mom's grave? I haven't been yet, and I think I feel strong enough to go today."

"I would be happy to go with you, hon. I will cut some flowers and bring with us. Would you like me to pick you up or meet you there?"

"I probably should ride with you. I have no idea how I will react. I have been numb. I haven't wanted to feel any more pressure or sadness. Mrs. Miller, do you have time to talk with me today? I need a mother's advice, and you are the nearest to a mother that I know. I've always referred to you as my second mother."

"And I've always considered you my daughter, Alivia. I can be with you as long as you like today. Why don't we just play it by ear and see what happens?"

"OK. That sounds good to me."

Alivia waited outside for Mrs. Miller. She didn't allow her to leave the vehicle but met her at the car.

Alivia reached over and gave Mrs. Miller a side hug. "Thank you so much. It means a lot to me that you would do this for me, all things considered."

"I've already told you, Alivia, that I harbor no resentment toward you at all. As a matter of fact, I discussed this very issue with Meagan before your wedding. She and I both agreed that it was probably best for you and Pete not to marry. You share a lifelong friendship, and I believe that both of you would have been unable to reach your full potential within the marriage.

"There is a lot more to marriage than friendship, Alivia. Much more. I'm very sorry that you did not get a chance to talk it out with your mother before the wedding. There was such a rush to get everything ready that there was no time available for discussions, plus the fact that you were trying to keep certain things from her."

"I have to wonder if I made the right choice, Mrs. Miller. My mom did not reap any benefits from my sudden marriage. She died despite our actions to protect her."

Mrs. Miller reached over to lay her hand over Alivia's. "Sugar, try to relax in the knowledge that God knows all things. His purpose will be carried out no matter what. I know you feel somewhat cheated by the outcome, but you can't see the end results. Who knows or can even guess what God has planned for your future? Think about this: what if God's plan has nothing to do with your mother and everything is about you? I must tell you Alivia, that in all of my reading and studying of the Word of God, I have found no scripture saying that God must answer our 'why' questions, nor does he consult us about the method he uses to accomplish his goal."

Alivia had no time to respond, as they had reached the cemetery. She didn't even know where her mother lay at rest but had to depend on Mrs. Miller to lead the way. As they approached the site, Alivia noticed that the dirt on the grave was still a mound. Time had not packed the dirt flat yet. What would this visit to the gravesite do for her?

She stood and looked down at the grave and tried to imagine her mother underground. She couldn't. She felt nothing. Her mind was blank. This was not what she had expected. She had thought that maybe if she saw the grave, she could more readily accept her mother's death. Why couldn't she cry? Why couldn't she fall over the grave and beat the earth? Why was she unable to produce any emotion? This trip was a big zero.

Alivia glanced around her at the multitude of grave markers. So many people to mourn. So many people whose lives had ended. What was the purpose for life anyway? Here today, gone tomorrow.

As she lay in her bed that night, her mind prompted her to review the words of wisdom she had received from Mrs. Miller. Could it be possible that this whole God thing was about her and not her mother? Were there lessons in God's silence? She wanted to know the answers, and reached into the nightstand for her Bible. She read and searched until she was too sleepy to hold her head up. But again, nothing concrete had jumped out at her as she had hoped. Could it be that the most important lesson for her was patience? Whatever the lesson was, she hoped she could learn it quickly and move on.

Chapter 48

Alivia decided she would try out Sir Lancelot. He should be relaxed enough after the transport for her to ride him. She quickly made her way to the stables and asked one of the hands to saddle him for her.

She allowed him to get her scent and stroked his face for a few minutes before she mounted. "You are a handsome fellow, Sir Lancelot. You have a lofty name, so I think I will call you 'Sir.' If you really are a bribe, you are a beautiful one. Now don't get a big ego just because I said you are handsome. Grandmother used to say, 'Handsome is as handsome does.'"

Alivia's spirits lifted as she felt the power of the horse beneath her. She loved horses more than almost any other thing. Horseback riding always calmed her when nothing else could.

As she had prepared to mount, she noticed that Sir was a little taller than Shadow, and that she had to stretch to the limit to get her foot into the stirrup. She had yet to meet a horse that she couldn't ride, but she used caution with Sir. They had to become familiar to each other before trust could be built, from each of them. Some horses were very sensitive and picked up on the rider's mood. She sure hoped Sir was not a moody animal. If he was, she would simply ride Shadow.

She easily guided Sir out of the stable grounds and once again turned her direction to her favorite place on the ranch. She had some thinking to do. Some planning.

Alivia was beginning to respond to Dayne and even to enjoy his visits. But she still had a long way to go before she moved back into the house with him. She admitted that she held him largely responsible for her condition. Why couldn't he have loaned Dad the money? Why did he want her? She didn't have the nerve to ask him these questions point blank.

Her real disappointment was with God. He could have kept her mother alive if he had wanted to. Why didn't he? Alivia felt that God had let her down big time, and she was less than eager to talk with him about it. Ha! God didn't have to respond to her at all. Apparently, he considered the subject closed. He certainly hadn't given her a new direction.

As a matter of fact, if he chose to speak audibly to her right now, she would still be leery of listening to him. Did God enjoy teasing his children? Did he really love her?

She had been through serious suffering and angst. How could God get pleasure from that?

God, I'm pretty sure I am not the only person to ask the question, "Why." I am really trying to recapture the love and trust that I once had for you. I surrendered all to you. I gave myself to you willingly. I don't need to list all the trials, all the sacrifice to you. You know all things.

As Alivia whispered her question to God, her thoughts took her back to the conversation she had with Mrs. Miller the day before. She had asked Alivia a question about roses and other fragrant flowers. When do you smell the most sweet-smelling aroma from these petals? It is when they are crushed that the scent is the strongest. The process of molding and shaping that God does in us is usually painful while he is using his tools, but the finished product is a vessel of honor; a vessel that God is proud to call his own.

If Alivia were completely honest, she would have to admit she felt a certain jealousy of Pete. He was excited and jubilant about his new love. When would it be her turn? Her husband made no false declarations of love to her, and she could not say that she loved him. As a matter of fact, she knew that she had intentionally hardened her heart toward him. Did she want him to suffer? She would not admit to such an accusation, even to herself.

Alivia wanted to feel elation, joy at the sound of her husband's voice. She wanted, no . . . needed, to feel that he cared for her. Her desire was to look forward to being with him, to enjoy being with him.

Her head drooped as she led Sir back to the stable. Tears were close, but she refused to allow them to flow. Sadness had a death grip on her, and she couldn't seem to care.

Chapter 49

Alivia decided to answer Morgan's call this time. For days she had ignored her friend's calls, telling herself that she would call Morgan later when she felt better.

"Hello, Morgan. I apologize for not taking your calls. I'm so sorry."

"Alivia, I love you. You are my best friend. Of course I worry about you and want you to recover fully from all that has happened in your life. Do you feel like company today?"

With a deep sigh, Alivia answered, "I suppose so. What do you have in mind?"

Morgan ignored her lukewarm reception and explained her plan. "I think that we should visit that new boutique on Main and Stella. I passed by a couple of days ago, and the dresses in the window look fabulous."

"Dresses? Really? It is already fall, Morgan. You know that I prefer pants anyway."

"Please, Alivia. Try to contain your excitement, will you? They have dresses with matching jackets for cool evenings. Also, friend, I have made an appointment with my hairdresser to have your hair worked on. You have let it go too long without attention."

Alivia gasped. "Morgan, you go too far. What if I like my hair like it is?"

"Oh, you mean dull and lifeless? Stringy dead ends? I think not, Alivia. Please allow me to have my way today, for old times' sake if nothing else."

"Morgan, I don't deserve your friendship. I have treated you abominably."

"Nonsense, girl. What are friends for if not to suffer a little abuse?"

She wasn't exactly excited to go, but Alivia gave in to her friend's wishes. The first stop was the hair salon where Morgan had already planned the treatment. She would have just a little highlight added to her beautiful honey-colored hair, as well as a cut.

Alivia watched the scissors in horror as the hairdresser snipped at the ends of her hair. She had to bite her tongue to keep her comments to herself. Would the girl cut all her hair off? When would she stop? Two hours later she was twirled around with a hand mirror to view the end results. She loved it! Wow, what a difference it made to her appearance.

With a smile on her face, Alivia spoke. "Morgan, I hate to admit it, but you were right. I love the way my hair looks. Thank you for using force to get me here."

"Think nothing of it. Now we'll have a look at the dresses."

With an eye roll, Alivia followed Morgan to the car.

At the entrance, a young woman approached them. "How may I assist you today?"

Morgan took over once again. "We would love to see your newest dresses in colors to complement my friend. I like the shades of blue that the mannequins are wearing. We may have to try different sizes. She has lost some weight, so we aren't sure about sizing."

"Follow me, and I'll get a dressing room ready for you. Let me know which dresses interest you, and I'll bring them to you in a couple of sizes."

After trying on a dozen or more dresses, Alivia chose to purchase three of them. Each had a cardigan or fitted jacket to match.

As they marched out of the store Morgan said, "Now for shoes."

Alivia gave a mock groan and allowed Morgan to lead the way.

Alivia's eyes landed on a pair of navy shoes with sassy straps across the foot and two-inch heels. She had to have them. Another pair in a bright blue caught her eye. She didn't wait for Morgan to lead her to the purses. It was time for a change.

Morgan wore a smirk as she dropped Alivia off at home. Mission accomplished.

Chapter 50

With her spirits lifted, Alivia decided a long soak in a bubble bath was required. She put a shower cap on her hair to keep it dry and filled the tub with water. She rested her head on a bathtub pillow and relaxed. She stayed in the bath until the water had cooled.

As she dried off, she looked at her body in the bathroom mirror. She had lost too much weight and was rail thin. She made the decision right then to begin to eat more.

She would not be wearing sandals but thought a new layer of nail polish on toes and hands would be a good idea. She chose a new color called Shrimp Devine.

With uncharacteristic boldness, she called Dayne. "Hi, are you busy?"

"I've told you before that I am never too busy for you. What's up?"

Alivia took a deep breath for courage and told him her thoughts. "I would like to go to Italiana's tonight. Do you think you can get reservations?"

Dayne answered with alacrity, in shock that she wanted to go out. "Yes dear, I can get reservations for tonight, even if I have to buy the restaurant. I'm excited that you feel up to an outing, Alivia. Especially as tonight was not on the schedule as a date night."

With a short gasp she answered, "Oh. I forgot. If you are busy, we can go another time."

"Not a chance. I will pick you up at seven." He hung up the phone with a grin on his face and a pep in his step.

Alivia had a hard time deciding which new dress to wear. She finally closed her eyes and grabbed one. She and Dayne were already married. Why did she feel so excited? She wasn't getting dressed for the senior prom, for goodness sake. She didn't mind these new emotions at all. Her stomach did a little flip when she thought of her husband. Would he like her new dress? Would he approve of the haircut? Would he even notice the changes? She was so confused at her hot and cold emotions. When would she be normal again?

Kenneth was in the family room when Alivia came downstairs. He sucked in a quick breath as he viewed her in her new clothes. "Alivia, I almost thought you were Meagan for a moment. You look delightful. I'm excited for you to show an interest in your appearance again."

Just as he walked across the room to give her a little kiss on the cheek, they heard a knock on the door. Kenneth was in position to see Dayne's reaction to his daughter as he entered the room. With a knowing smile, he greeted him.

Dayne stood rooted to the spot, eyes focused on Alivia. His heart began pounding in his chest, and he could scarcely get his breath. "Alivia. Alivia."

Kenneth laughed at the young man. "Yes, Dayne, she is Alivia. Come on in."

Dayne felt like a gangly teen on his first date. Where did his confidence go? Where was the smooth charm he had always used at countless events? Finally, he shook himself out of the shock that held his tongue as prisoner.

"Alivia, you are gorgeous. Did you do something different to your hair? You look fabulous in that dress. The color is becoming." He took a full breath. "I am very happy to see you looking so well. You have made a giant step forward, sweetheart."

Dayne could barely contain his excitement and hopes for the evening. He had been elated when Alivia called him and had kept his fingers crossed all afternoon that she would not cancel the appointment.

As they exited the car in front of the restaurant, Dayne offered Alivia his arm. She looked up into his face and smiled as she placed her hand on his arm. He tossed the car key to the valet and escorted his lovely wife inside.

Each stared at the other across the table, thoughts whirling through their heads.

Alivia began her new pledge to eat more by ordering the indescribably delicious lasagna with garlic bread and regular salad dressing on her salad. She would see after she had eaten her fill whether to order dessert.

Dayne could barely eat his meal for staring at his wife. He was unaware of other people in the restaurant. His hopes were high about the ending of this evening. Could this be the beginning of a new chapter for them?

He remembered none of their conversation, but he did cherish the smiles Alivia had thrown his way.

As they reached the ranch, he decided he would go in with her for a while. He hurried to the passenger side to help her out of the car.

Alivia gave a groan. "Why did you let me eat that dessert by myself? I am so full. Next time you must promise to eat your share or I won't have any either. You, sir, are no gentleman."

A laugh escaped his lips before he could call it back. "I believe the question is, 'Are you a lady?'"

She gave him a friendly glare. "A gentleman never disagrees with a lady."

Alivia's first action after entering the room was to slip out of her shoes. "Ooh, how good that feels. I really dislike shoes. You should try to remember this information so you will be prepared in the future for possible embarrassment."

His ears latched onto the words "in the future" and his heart almost stopped beating. "Wife, you could never embarrass me, whatever you do. I want you to always feel comfortable with me and be yourself. You don't have to act for me."

"Thank you, husband. I will try to behave, at least in public."

He had not planned to do it, but he could not seem to stop himself. He pulled her close and kissed her tenderly and slowly. With the barest whisper he said, "I think I had better leave now, or I won't be able to leave at all." His lips left her mouth and traced her neck and jawline. Would she ask him to stay? Could he bear it if she didn't?

"Dayne? Are you in a hurry?"

"No. Definitely not."

"Is it possible for you to stay with me tonight? It's OK if you can't. I'll understand."

"Are you kidding? I would never turn down an invitation from you, Alivia."

As he followed her from the room, he floated behind her. His heart almost burst with love for her. Soon he would tell her. Soon.

Chapter 51

Dayne woke slowly, savoring every moment of lying next to Alivia. He hated to move a muscle, afraid she would wake up and then be gone from his arms. He loved her more with every passing day. He prayed that she would come to terms with her mother's death soon. He wanted her to be with him every day, not sometimes.

He reminded himself that she was several years younger than he and thought she had handled herself well considering the chaos she had endured. He had to question his own motives. Had he done the right thing by practically forcing her to marry him? Was he at least partly responsible for her state of mind? He was ready to move on. What a callous thought! He would continue to move slowly and allow Alivia to set the pace.

Their relationship had improved since she had moved back to Kenneth's ranch. He had hope for their future together. He dreamed of little girls who looked like a copy of Alivia. They had not had time to discuss the possibility of such plans before life got crazy and she was so ill.

He pulled her closer to him as he thought of how close he had come to losing her before they could even begin a life together. *Thank you, God.*

Alivia stirred and turned to face him. She opened her eyes and stared at him a moment before she gave him a sleepy smile and wished him a good morning.

"I'm glad you stayed last night. I had a wonderful evening with you. I felt a little like Cinderella, but you didn't leave me when I lost my shoes." Her smile was sincere.

"No, I didn't leave you. I will never leave you, Alivia."

She searched his eyes for the truth. Her emotions were everywhere. Why couldn't she forgive his part in the trauma she called her life? She wanted to be at peace with him and with herself.

"Dayne, I want to discuss something with you. Please hear me out before you decide. On second thought, let's wait until after we are dressed and have eaten breakfast before we talk. I've always heard that the way to a man's heart is through his stomach."

He answered with a smile. How he wanted to tell her that she already owned his heart. But not yet. The time wasn't right.

He kissed her lightly and sprang from the bed. "Come on then, lazy bones. We can't eat until you get out of that bed."

Kenneth had left for work about an hour earlier, so they had the kitchen to themselves. He started the coffee brewing while she rummaged in the refrigerator. "I have eggs and cheese. How about an omelet? Or I could cook you something a little more substantial. Your call."

"Omelets sound fine to me. Do you know how to cook, Alivia?"

She turned to look at him and pretended to be offended. "I'll have you know I am a good cook. My mother thought every woman should be able to cook more than cookies."

"Sorry. I didn't mean to rile you up. Not on such a beautiful day. Not on a day when we are getting along so well." He stepped across the kitchen and took her in his arms.

She swatted him away. "We will never get anything to eat if you don't behave, mister."

He chuckled and let her go. "You win. This time."

After they had eaten, they each took a mug of coffee out to the side porch where the view was pretty special. She had spent a lot of time on that porch. Most of the memories were shared with Pete. Pete. Maybe she sabotaged herself with her thoughts. She refused to get sidetracked with negativity.

She took a sip of coffee and looked him in the eye. "I want to run an idea by you. It seems to me that I can accept our marriage better from this vantage point. I can't really explain it, but I feel suffocated at your house. Being here where I grew up helps me to relax and allows me to feel OK with who I am. Do you think I am being childish?"

"No, you aren't childish. You have had some serious things to deal with all within a short span of time. You will not be critical of yourself, Alivia."

"Thank you. Would it be possible for you to bring some of your things out here for just a short while? I know I am asking a lot, so if you aren't willing to work with my plan, please tell me the truth."

"Alivia, sweetheart, I will make whatever arrangements you think are necessary to please you. I want you to be happy, Alivia. If you can't come to me, then I certainly will come to you. Do you think Kenneth will mind my being here?"

"Ha! Are you kidding? He will love it. Oh, wait. That would mean that I have two men in the house fussing over me like a mother hen. I may want to rethink this idea."

With a wide smile he replied, "Oh no you don't. You have issued an invitation, and I accepted. No going back on your word." He stood and held out his hands to her. "Come, Mrs. Travers. Let us seal the deal." He touched her face with a soft caress before he placed his lips on hers.

Alivia leaned into him and allowed herself to relax and enjoy her husband's affection. For today. For this moment.

Chapter 52

After Dayne left her, Alivia called Natalie. "Nat, I think it is about time for you to bring the boys out for another riding lesson. I know you don't care for horses, but Parker and Peyton do. Do you think you could bring them to the ranch today?"

"Well, well, little sister. Your mood seems to have improved since I last saw you. What, or should I say who, has had this impact on you?" She teased.

"Cut it out, Nat. I do feel good today, but don't you start pressing me. I just feel like spending time with my boys. They need to be outside so they can enjoy this beautiful weather before it gets cold. What do you say?"

"OK, sis. I can be there in a couple of hours. They do need to get out and run off some energy. Those two wear me out. It's like they get supercharged, but I don't."

Alivia chuckled as she pictured the twins. They did seem to be extra active, but they were also extra special. "I'll have the ponies ready for them. Joe and the other hands keep them exercised, so they won't be too wild for the boys to handle. "

Alivia met the group outside as they pulled into the drive. She opened the door and started helping them get unbuckled. "Auntie! Auntie! Mom said you called and 'vited us to come ride the horses. It'll be so much fun! Mom also said to mind our manners. What does that mean?"

Laughing, Alivia grabbed them both for hugs and kisses. "Are you two up for a picnic today? I thought we would ride out to the pond and have lunch under my favorite tree."

"Yes. Yes."

"Payton, Parker, come with me to the stables. I have someone for you to meet." She led them to the stall where Sir Lancelot lived. "What do you think? Is he beautiful or what?"

"No, Auntie. He isn't beautiful; he's handsome. Boys are handsome."

"Well, excuse me, Parker. You are right. He is handsome. He is a gift from Uncle Dayne. Do you like him? Maybe one day you will be able to ride him."

As she watched the boys eyeing the horse, she couldn't stop herself from imagining little boys who looked just like Dayne. Whoa! She was not ready to go there.

Without realizing that Natalie had followed them to the stables, Alivia was unprepared for Natalie's observation. "Well, Alivia, it seems to me that a certain someone has found a way to make brownie points. That is a magnificent animal."

She whirled around with a mock glare for Natalie. "Yes, and another certain someone should mind her own business, or I might throw her across his back and let her have a wild ride."

Throwing her hands up in surrender, Natalie answered, "No ride for me, thanks. I'll go in and look over my new magazine. There are some really cute fall arrangements in it that I believe I can copy." She did not speak her thoughts aloud, but she was thrilled to get a little alone time. She adored her boys, but a break away from them wouldn't hurt her.

Alivia got the boys situated on their ponies and mounted Shadow. "Boys, follow me. I mean it! You must not try to ride faster than I allow. Promise me."

"We promise. We'll be good, Auntie."

"I have a surprise for you at the pond."

Both boys yelled out, "What is it?"

"If I tell you now, it won't be a surprise. You'll just have to wait and see."

Alivia took them riding around the pasture for about an hour, and then headed toward the pond where she had the picnic supplies and fishing poles waiting for them.

"I thought you boys might like to do a little fishing today. I have the poles and plenty of big juicy worms for us to use. The pond has plenty of catfish and bream so you should be able to catch some. I'll cook them for you."

"Auntie, you're the best!" They seemed to forget all about lunch in their excitement to begin fishing.

After many grubby worms and wild casting, Parker finally landed a fish. Alivia and Peyton yelled, "Bring him in, Park, bring him in."

Yes, he did bring him in. Parker was so excited to have a fish hanging at the end of his pole that he forgot how to get him to the bank. He jerked wildly and slapped Alivia right in the face with the fish. Unfortunately, the hook caught in Alivia's hair and held tight. Luckily, it was a small bream. Alivia rummaged through the tackle box for clippers to cut the line. She would have to wear the fish home.

No one in the house could miss the fact that the boys were back. They went into the house yelling, "Mommy, Mommy, come quick. We went fishing, and Auntie has the fish stuck in her hair. Come see, Mommy. Come see."

The boys were doubled over in laughter. Peyton spoke up, "Auntie, you have a fish for an earring!"

Natalie stepped into the room and stood still in shock. She burst into uncontrollable laughter as she grabbed her phone for a picture. "Alivia, this is one for the books. I can use this picture for blackmail in the future."

"What is going on in here?" Dayne and Kenneth heard the giggling and came to investigate. They stopped in their tracks as they viewed the scene before them. They tried to control their mirth but lost the battle.

Alivia glared at them, but they didn't stop laughing. Dayne motioned for someone to come forward. "Alivia, I'd like to introduce you to Detective Phil Morgan."

With as much dignity as she could muster, Alivia lifted her chin and said calmly, "So nice to meet you detective. If you'll excuse me, I will go and change into something a little more appropriate." As she slipped by her husband she whispered into his ear, "You are a dead man."

Dayne followed her. "Do you think you might need help getting the hook untangled?"

"Can you take the time from the party? I wouldn't want you to miss anything on my account."

"Oh, believe me, I haven't missed a thing." Turning to their guest he said, "Phil, I won't be gone long. It seems that my wife is a little tied up and needs my help."

Giggles followed them out of the room.

In less than an hour, Alivia reappeared in clean, non-fishy clothes and hair washed and dried. Her look dared Dayne to say a word although she had a difficult time holding her own laughter.

Dayne and Phil exchanged looks, both smiling.

"Alivia, Phil has asked that you go to the police station tomorrow and view the men in a lineup. Do you think you can handle that? Of course, they won't be able to see you."

"Yes, I think so. I am ready to be told a few facts about the episode. My mind is so unclear over the details that I don't know what was real and what I dreamed. At least the nightmares have stopped. I'm thankful for that."

Shaking Dayne's hand once more, Phil left them with plans to see them the next morning.

Chapter 53

Alivia thought she had her nerves under control as she entered the police station. Phil met them and led them back to the observation room, where six men stood in a line facing them.

As she looked over the men, her voice shook slightly as she pointed to the second man from the left. "He was one of them. He is the one who forced me to write the note, and he is the one who taped me with duct tape. I didn't really get a good look at the other two, but I'm sure there were three."

Leaving the prisoners, they all returned to Phil's office before anyone spoke. Alivia was first to break the silence. With a deep breath she said, "Detective, could you please fill me in on some of the details? I have scraps of memory, but I don't know what is real or what my numbed mind thought up. I seem to have a little niggling thought of some huge black man. I think he called himself Tank. Is he real?"

"Yes, Alivia, he is real. He took you to the hospital and pretty much saved your life. Do you remember the sequence of events?"

Alivia bit her bottom lip as she tried to focus. "I was pumping gas when someone grabbed me and flung me into a vehicle. My head hit something, and I was unconscious for a time. When I came to, I realized we were moving, but I had no clue what direction we were going. I kept quiet and didn't let them know that I had regained consciousness.

"I seem to recall an abandoned shed of some kind. It reeked of rotted vegetation and mildew. I had difficulty breathing. The man I showed you in the lineup was the one to throw me into the old shed. He didn't tie me up at first, and I had a chance to look around. At least as much as I could as the moon was the only light I had. I noticed a big hole in the back wall where the wood had rotted. I planned to smash into the wall and make the hole bigger if I had the slightest chance.

"The men all seemed to be drinking. They laughed and talked like they were at a party. Then the big guy came back to me and gave me paper and pencil and demanded me to write what he said. I asked for water, but he sneered and said no."

Closing her eyes and breathing deeply, she continued her tale with a quivering voice. "That is when he taped me. I knew my chances for escape had narrowed to practically zero. I worked and worked to get my boots off. Probably the only reason I was successful was the fact that I had worn thinner socks that made the boots a little looser.

"I began to lose consciousness after that. I guess I had used up what little energy I had getting rid of my boots. I don't know how many hours passed before I came to. The combination of exhaustion and dehydration made me helpless.

"I did realize that I had to move if I were to live. At some point the men must have all fallen asleep. I went to the back wall and pushed against the flimsy wall and was able to get out of the shed.

"I was disoriented and had no idea which direction I should go." Alivia was totally unaware that tears slipped down her face as she spoke of the awful trauma she had endured. She sucked in another breath before she spoke again.

"I remember praying and asking God to lead me in the right path. I began to walk as quickly as possible with the darkness and no boots. I tried to put as much distance as possible between the men and me.

"At some point I stumbled and fell. Unable to break the fall, my head struck something hard. I couldn't go another inch. I laid there until the sun lit my surroundings, and then I forced myself to get up and keep walking. I am not clear about what happened next."

Phil waited to allow Dayne to pick up the story. "Phil called in the K-9 unit to trail you. They led us to the spot where you fell. When I saw blood on the trail, I thought the worst. After sniffing the blood, the dogs set out again and led us to an opening in the woods where they found your jacket."

Dayne was almost overcome with emotion as he recalled the scene. His feet moved him across the room of their own volition. He grasped her hands, needing the physical connection to her. "Alivia, when I saw your jacket soaked in blood, I thought I would pass out. Phil searched the area for clues. The only detail that made any sense was that someone took you away on a motorcycle. There was evidence that several bikes had been there recently. The tracks were easy to trail.

"Phil spotted an oil trail and we discussed following it. He sent other men and called in officers from the nearest towns for assistance. The oil dribble led us to a small town about ten miles back toward Dallas. We tracked it to a small hospital and rushed in to question the employees, hoping to find you there. They were unable to identify you and had sent you to another clinic.

"By the time we arrived, you had already been airlifted to Dallas General. We found Tank there, and he verified our theory about the group on motorcycles. He is the hero, Alivia. He brought you into town on his motorcycle, and from what the employees said, he demanded treatment for you.

"I'll never be able to thank him enough, Alivia. I have every intention of keeping in touch with him; and in the very near future, I plan to reward him in some way. I'll have to be sneaky, though. He is a proud man and a great Christian to boot. He told me that God had directed him, and he was in that exact position to help you."

Alivia asked, "Would it be possible for me to meet him? I would so like to thank him personally."

"Sweetheart, I would love for you to see him. I'll call and plan a day that is convenient for him. You should see for yourself how God kept his hand on you even through such a tumultuous time."

Alivia's only answer was a smile.

Chapter 54

D ayne left Alivia with a kiss and a promise to return shortly. She saw that she had received a notification from Natalie. Nat's message said to call her.

"Hi, sister. What's up?"

With a loud noise in the background, Natalie spoke over it. "Alivia, in all of the turmoil the past few months, I totally forgot to tell you that I had picked up your wedding photos. Do you feel like coming over to look at them?"

With a chuckle she answered, "Nat, a visit to the zoo would cheer me up tremendously. Those two monkeys of yours always make me feel like a million bucks. They are stinkers, no doubt, but they are sweet stinkers."

She left immediately and headed to Natalie's home. Were the fall colors more vibrant than usual? She also questioned the smooth ride. Had Dayne put new shocks on her car or what? She rolled down the windows and enjoyed the slightly nippy air that whirled through her car.

Dayne. She felt their relationship changing, but where was it leading? Had she come to care for her husband? She wished she could let go of his part in the whole bitter circumstances of her mother's death. If there weren't so many factors in the situation, she thought she could fall in love with her husband. Oh well, she couldn't figure out her whole life in a few minutes.

In next to no time she arrived at Natalie's place. Of course, the twins ran out to meet her.

"Hi, monkeys! You seem a little extra exuberant today."

"What's zuberant?" Parker and his questions.

"It means lively and energetic. Maybe it means that you two should ride your bikes for a while so I can talk to your mommy. After that, I have a new story for you.

She and Natalie looked at them and shook their heads. Natalie spoke up, "If I had a fraction of their energy, I could accomplish a lot. Come on in. I already have the coffee ready; and believe it or not, I have a fresh cake that is still warm."

"Wow. I am impressed, big sister. You can watch the monkeys and still bake? You are a woman of many talents."

Natalie stared at Alivia until Alivia asked if she had something on her face. "No, nothing on your face but a sweet smile. It seems you are gradually getting better. I'm so glad, sis. The whole family has prayed and prayed for you."

"Thank you, Nat. I do feel better. Actually, I want to discuss something with you—Dayne. I realize I am holding on with a tight fist to a grudge against him. I have prayed about it, but the problem persists."

Natalie thought for a moment before answering. "Alivia, honey, the Bible teaches us to be patient in tribulation and to persist in prayer. In Romans he tells us to be transformed by the renewing of our mind. Also, in John he said that in this life we will have trouble but be courageous because he has conquered the world.

"Do you remember the verses we had to memorize in our Girl's Impact class? 'Whatsoever things are true, whatsoever things are lovely . . . '"

"'Think on these things.' I know, I know," Alivia said.

"I think I will listen to scripture on the way home. I need to revisit some of these passages in the Word. I know God is not pleased with me when I intentionally hold onto this anger toward my husband.

"The thing is, I think I would be OK if only I could have told Mom goodbye. This is a major hang-up for me. It seems that I must overcome this attitude to move forward.

"I will admit to you that Dayne is a great person. He treats me with such kindness and patience. I would have already given up on me if I were Dayne."

Natalie smiled. "I want to show you the wedding pictures and then hear your comments. I believe you will be surprised by what the photos reveal."

"What do you mean?"

"Not telling. You will see for yourself."

As Alivia viewed the pictures, she relived her wedding day. She remembered her excitement even though she was not marrying Dayne out of love. She could see happiness in her face. Happiness? Even then? She looked slowly and methodically at each photo. In one shot Dayne looked down at her face while she was looking elsewhere. What she saw shocked her. It appeared his eyes showed love. How confusing! It was not possible that he could have loved her when he married her.

Alivia did not believe in love at first sight. Attraction, yes, but love? No. She admitted to herself that she felt attraction from the first moment they had met. Could a couple have a successful marriage based on physical attraction?

"Nat, what I see is impossible. My eyes must be playing tricks on me. He can't love me. We've barely had any time to get to know each other, with all the ruckus of the kidnapping and Mom's death. How could it be, Nat?"

"I can't explain it, Alivia. Why don't you discuss this with him? He is the only person who can satisfy your questions."

Alivia's head jerked up. "You've got to be kidding me. I can't just walk up to him and ask him if he loves me. I can't do it, Nat."

"Silly girl. Of course not. There will be a right time for the questions, but until that time, please keep focused on the scripture verses we talked about."

"Thanks, Nat. I will. I suppose I must allow Dayne to see this album."

Natalie laughed. "Think fast because I see the two little tornados heading our way."

Chapter 55

Dayne called around two o'clock to ask Alivia if she could get ready to go out for dinner. He had a special person that he wanted her to meet.

"Who is it? Do I know this person?"

"I should keep you in suspense, but I'll have mercy on you and tell you that the guest is Tank. You mentioned that you would like to meet him in person, so I invited him to have dinner with us tonight."

"That sounds great, Dayne. But can't you just bring him home with you this evening? We could have a private visit with him in our home. I would love to cook a good meal for him. Do you think he will come?"

"Probably. I'll check with him and see what he thinks. He is an amazing man, Alivia. Naturally, I appreciate what he did for you, but in a lot of other ways he is exceptional. You'll see what I mean when you have talked with him for a few minutes."

Alivia thought for a moment before she asked Dayne to ask what Tank's favorite dessert was. She wanted to do something nice for him. From all accounts, she owed her very life to him.

She busied herself with dinner plans, checking the pantry and the freezer to make sure she had all the ingredients she needed. She called Dayne for more information. "Dayne, please check with Tank and find out if he has any allergies, or preferences regarding meat choice. There are a lot of things to consider when cooking for someone special."

"Oh, I see. I don't recall you ever asking me for my preferences. I guess you don't consider me special enough." Dayne teased her.

Alivia burst into laughter. "Oops!" She giggled all afternoon. She was prepared for dinner on schedule and waited patiently for her husband to get home and met him at the door.

As Dayne stepped to the side and began to introduce her to Tank, she threw herself at Tank. "Thank you, thank you for helping me. I can barely remember the incident, but I thought I remembered something about a big man with warm brown eyes." She had to stand on her toes to reach him. "I hope I never forget you. I owe you my life. My husband has told me a little about you, but I want to know you for myself."

Dayne stood by in silence watching his beautiful wife hugging on another man. He felt no ill will, though. Truthfully, he wanted to hug Tank himself. The memory of his helplessness had not quite been erased. Many times Dayne had to shift his thoughts to prevent panic from taking over.

Alivia blushed a little as she led the way to the family room. "Dad should be in shortly. He went to check the stables. After the awful experience we had recently, he keeps a closer watch on our horses."

Tank spoke up. "Do you mind if I look? I used to love riding."

Dayne offered to show him the way while Alivia finished up the last touches for dinner.

The men carried on a lively conversation as they ate the delicious meal. Alivia watched them mostly in silence. After dessert she asked to speak with Tank privately.

While Dayne and Kenneth cleaned up the kitchen, Alivia led Tank into a small sitting room nearby. "Tank, thank you for your kindness to me. I was at the end of my endurance when I fell into your group. I don't remember anyone but you, Tank. I would like to ask you about the peace you exhibited. I don't think I have ever seen eyes like yours. Do you know Jesus?"

Tank gave her a brilliant smile as he answered. "Mrs. Travers, Jesus is my constant companion. I have had to lean on him a lot the last few years."

"I am a Christian too, but I don't seem to have the level of peace that I see in you. Do you have a secret that you can share? Before you answer, please call me Alivia."

Tank slowly shook his head. "There is no secret, Alivia. I believe the Word of God. All of it. There are many scriptures about peace, but in order to live in peace, we must embrace what the Word says. There are no shortcuts. We must surrender completely to God and allow him access to areas of our lives that we sometimes want to reserve for ourselves."

Alivia thought for a moment before saying anything. "I thought I had surrendered to Christ completely until my mother became ill. I did something that I thought was in God's will, but it seems that maybe I was in my own will."

"Why are you confused? Has something happened to make you doubt God's directive?"

"Sort of. I mean, things have not turned out the way they were supposed to go, so I must have mistaken God's wishes. I try to live a life pleasing to him, and I was sure that God wanted me to do this certain thing. But instead of improving the situation, it seems to have backfired."

Tank rubbed his chin as if in deep thought. "OK, Alivia, let me get this straight. You felt compelled to do a certain thing— an urging you were sure came from God. Did God speak to your heart and let you know that he had changed his mind?"

"Oh no. I just expected different results from my obedience to him. I prayed for something to happen, and he didn't do what I asked. I made a serious sacrifice for someone, and I feel that God didn't keep his end of the deal. I'm pretty sure you are shocked by this confession."

"Not shocked, no. But I am a little puzzled by what you have told me. Do you believe that you made a bargain with God? A trade for answered prayer in exchange for your obedience?"

Biting her thumbnail, she felt shame. "That sounds a little harsh, don't you think? I didn't deliberately set out to make a trade with God, but I did feel and still do feel that he got the best of the deal. I mean, I made the sacrifice to please him, and he didn't deliver what he promised."

"Alivia, did God actually give you a promise? Tell me exactly how this played out. I must understand what you believe in order to help you to understand. Did you surrender your wishes to him for the sole purpose of obedience to God? Or did you sacrifice your will for someone other than God? For a family member or even for yourself? What was your motivation for the sacrifice?"

Caught off guard by the questions, Alivia had no quick answer for Tank's questions. "I don't know, Tank. I guess I need to search my heart. I do know that I have a little bitterness to overcome. I know what the Bible says about holding a grudge and allowing a seed of unforgiveness to grow."

"Alivia, if you want the peace of God that transcends all understanding, you must rid your heart of all malice, jealously, and envy. Go to God with a clean and willing heart. The Spirit of the Living God dwells in you to help you have the strength you need to accomplish this. I will tell you straight up, Alivia, that you must surrender completely to him. All self-will must go.

"Alivia, there are two words that carry a heavy weight. The first is 'I.' I this, I that. Everything is all about me, what I want, what I should do or not do, how I should benefit. The other word is 'if.' If only this and that, if only I had done, if only he had. These two small words will control your mind if you allow it. There are twenty-six letters in our alphabet. Try to use these two letters as little as possible.

"You know, Alivia, some people think of God as a great big Santa in the sky waiting to send us what we want. That belief is a lie. He is a righteous and holy God, a God who demands a high standard of living. A jealous and powerful God.

"Alivia, have you studied the gospels to find out exactly how Jesus lived those brief years here on earth? He repeatedly said that he had not come to do his will but the will of the Father. He told masses as he taught them that he only said what the Father had told him to say. Even the life-changing sacrifice Jesus made on the cross was not his will but the Father's. He asked the Father if it were possible to please let the cup pass from him, but nevertheless, not his will but the Father's be done. His death on the cross is how God had planned the reconciliation of men to God, but also Jesus did this as an act of obedience to the Father.

"I am going to ask you a difficult question, Alivia. A question that you may not be ready to answer right away without thinking it over. This act of obedience that you mentioned—did you perform this act in obedience to God for the sole purpose of pleasing him? Or did you do it in expectation of God allowing your will to override his will?"

"Thank you, Tank. I will certainly have something to chew on for a few days. You have given me direction. I will spend some serious time with my Bible tonight, and on my knees."

"Don't thank me, Alivia. Thank God. I speak and do what I believe God tells me to say and do. Nothing is done on my own. I went through great trials and tribulation to get to the place I am in now. I had bitterness against my wife, against God, against the marines. I felt abused and abandoned by them all. I was in a foxhole when I fully gave all the problems to God and totally surrendered my life to him. I wouldn't allow myself to be taken from this life with all the darkness that had invaded my heart. I could take you right to the spot where I gave myself to God. He dropped peace and calmness into my soul, my spirit, my heart. I left that foxhole a new man."

"I'm so glad for you, Tank. Thank you for talking to me with honesty. I suppose we had better join the other men before they send a search party for us." With a smile on her face, she stood to join her husband and father.

When it was time for Tank to leave, they all begged him to stay in touch. Dayne mentioned something about finding the exact job that would fit Tank. "I know, I know. You have already explained to me that you must seek God first and see what he wants you to do. I sure hope that he has a mind for you to be on board with me. I'll walk you to your car."

Chapter 56

S urprisingly, Alivia woke up the next morning feeling more anxiety than she had felt in months. She questioned Dayne's motivation in giving Sir Lancelot to her. Was he trying to buy her love? Or did he even care whether she loved him? What was the real reason he was being so accommodating? How much longer could she stand these yo-yo emotions?

She thought that she would feel differently after that long talk with Tank the night before. She had spent a lot of time with her Bible, as she had told Tank that she would do. She had also prayed, and thought she had everything under control.

She jumped into her clothes and headed downstairs. Luckily, she had the house to herself this morning. It would be impossible for her to be civil to the men. Oh, why couldn't her moods stabilize?

With jaws clenched, she filled the coffee pot and measured out the coffee for a strong brew. She needed something to energize her. She longed for something but couldn't decide what that something was.

While waiting for the coffee, she searched the pantry for pancake mix. Pancakes and bacon sounded good. The ringing of her phone interrupted her train of thought. It was Dayne. Trying to make her voice pleasant, she answered. "Hello, Dayne."

"Good morning, wife. I am calling to let you know that I will need to stay in town for two or three days. I have several early meetings, and it will be more convenient for me to be here rather than the ranch. Will this arrangement be OK with you?"

"Of course, Dayne. Do what you need to do. I need to go back to the house at some point and retrieve a few more personal things. I'll try to catch up with you."

"That sounds good, Alivia. I'll keep in touch."

Alivia poured herself a mug of coffee, taking a couple of blissful sips. Brain spinning in every direction, she thought to call Natalie. "Nat, I need help. I've had a bad start to the day. I am so confused. I can't stand it anymore!" She burst into tears and blubbered her frustrations to Nat.

Nat listened patiently while her sister vented her frustration. "Alivia, can you tell me what has you so upset? What are you confused about?"

"Oh Nat, I'm not sure. The only thing I am certain of is that I am unhappy, discontented, and that something must change with me. I can't stand the roller coaster moods another minute. Why can't I move on, Nat?"

"Honey, I wish I could tell you. I am not a trained counselor, but I can give you what sisterly advice I have. From my perspective it seems as though you don't believe you deserve to be happy. Maybe you feel guilty about breaking up with Peter, or just maybe you are dumping condemnation on yourself because you have romantic feelings for your husband."

"You are kidding me, right? Nat, how can you suggest such a thing?" Alivia fumed.

"What thing are you referring to, Alivia? Guilt or the fact that you have had a change of heart toward Dayne?"

"Natalie!"

"Maybe, Alivia, you can't rid yourself of the jealousy you feel toward Pete. I mean, the fact that he found someone else to love so quickly after the breakup. Do you have envy in your heart? Or maybe your feelings are hurt because you thought Pete would grieve for a very long time?"

Alivia huffed into the phone. "Well, please forgive me for placing my burdens on you, sister. It seems that you have made up your mind that I am a shallow and vain person who cannot play the cards dealt to her."

"Not so, Alivia. Not at all. But I do feel that you have wallowed and enjoyed your pity party long enough and need to get on with your life. You have a wonderful family who has stood with you through all your trials and chaos. We felt pain right along with you. We were scared out of our minds when you were kidnapped. Are you so centered on your own pain that you can't understand the pain of others or even acknowledge that we hurt?"

Silent, Alivia looked at the phone. She was bereft of words to say to her sister. Did Nat speak truth to her? Could these accusations possibly be real?

Natalie continued berating her little sister. "Have you given any thought to the fact that we are all mourning the death of Mom? Dad has dealt with the loss of his wife as well as the stress of your kidnapping. We all have had a hard time, Alivia. And what about Dayne? Have you given the least consideration to him? Do you think he is going to treat you like fine china forever? Do you have any plans for the future of your marriage, Alivia? How long are you going to loll around like a spoiled teenager who didn't get what she wanted?"

Dumbfounded, Alivia finally found her voice. "Natalie, do you really believe what you are saying? Do you think I want to be depressed and moody just to gain attention?"

"No, of course not, Alivia. I'm merely pointing out that you need to be honest with yourself about your feelings for Dayne and about Pete too. 'To thine own self be true.' Dig and stir around in your heart and see what comes to the surface. You could be surprised."

"Nat, I truly believe I have a right to be upset and maybe a little angry with God. I have lost the complete trust that I once had for him. I don't know what to expect from him anymore."

With a sigh, Natalie answered, "Do you want to be right, Alivia, or to have the right relationship with God? Only you can answer this question. Think about it, sis."

Alivia no longer wanted pancakes and bacon, but she did refill her coffee mug. She sat and pondered the things Natalie had thrown at her. Wow. She would think twice before calling her again.

With a heavy heart Alivia went to the stable and saddled up Shadow. A good ride always improved her disposition. For some reason she could think more clearly from the back of her horse. Was that normal? Reaching her favorite place on the ranch, Alivia dismounted and found a shady place to sit under her tree.

An inky blackness wrapped around her with heavy tentacles. A blackness so thick she could feel it pressing against her. She could barely get a breath, and when she did, she gagged on the putrid smell of evil. She could see nothing, not even a tiny ray of light. The blackness tried to squeeze the life from her as a boa constrictor wraps around its prey. She felt the fear and panic rise in her throat, choking out the life-giving air. Where was she? She began to scream with the little breath she did have. Help! Someone help.

Alivia jerked awake to find herself leaning against the tree. Sweat poured from her face as she sucked in a deep breath and tried to shake off the desperation of the nightmare. Falling to her knees, she sobbed her heart out to God. "Jesus, I want you. I need you. Please forgive me for allowing your presence to be smothered by my own stubbornness. Please shine your light in all the dark places of my heart and refresh my spirit. I can't live without you, Jesus. I know your power can release me from the darkness I allowed to come into my heart. Jesus, I am so sorry!"

A welcome peace flowed into and through her, chasing all darkness from her. She sat with her eyes closed, head tilted toward the heavens, and basked in the sweet and holy presence that replaced the evil that had taken up residence in her heart. She sat for a long time, content to be still in God's presence, to allow her spirit to be nourished and her soul refreshed.

Gazing at the clouds, a sudden memory floated through her mind. *I must go, punkin. It is not time for you yet. Embrace your journey and live.* Alivia bolted to her feet. What? Where did that come from? With clear vision she remembered. Her mother had kissed her on her cheek and said those words to her. But how? When? She had to talk to her dad. Now. She grabbed her phone and called him. She must know.

"Dad? I must ask you a question, a very important question. Did I die or almost die at any point during my recovery from the abduction? Please, Dad, give me the truth."

Silence reigned.

"Dad! I have to know!"

Finally, she heard her dad's voice, low but audible. "Yes, honey, you did die. The doctor at the clinic said that they had to work hard to keep you with us. The timing was right before you were airlifted to the Dallas General. What made you think to ask this?"

Tears flowing freely, Alivia answered, "Oh, Dad. I have something to tell you but not now, not on the phone. I'll see you later this evening and tell you my story."

Alivia sat with knees bent, elbows resting on them, with her head in her hands. She did get to say goodbye to her mother. All this time she had wasted fretting! Her mother kissed her goodbye before she went to heaven. Her heart almost burst from her body. An unnatural calmness descended on her as the memory gained momentum.

She had to go to town at once. She must share this memory with Dad first, and then with Dayne. She raced back to the house with a song in her heart.

Chapter 57

After an intense emotional session with her father, Alivia entered Dayne's house and was immediately drawn to the aroma of freshly brewed coffee. She thought Lena had Wednesdays off. As she approached the family room, she stopped dead in her tracks. There was a woman sitting on the sofa, alone, sipping coffee.

Startled, Alivia spoke. "Who are you? How did you get in?"

The woman casually answered. "I am Selena, and I let myself in with my key."

"Your key?" Alivia became more puzzled by the minute.

Serena smiled. "Yes, my key. Dayne gave it to me."

Temper flared in Alivia's chest and she gave way to it. "Give it to me," she demanded.

Still smiling, Selena spoke. "I don't think so, honey. I may need it again. Oh, are you Dayne's little bride? I heard that he had married a young girl. He will soon tire of you, you know. He is accustomed to socializing with the elite of Dallas society. I don't believe he will be content with such an innocent as you for long."

Nostrils flaring, Alivia spat the words through clenched teeth. "Give. Me. The. Key. Hand it over right now or I'll take it by force. You have no need of a key to this house. Whether or not my husband gave it to you, I am taking it."

No longer smiling, Selena stood. She eyed Alivia as if sizing her up. "I don't think you can take it from me, honey. You may as well accept the fact that Dayne is a man of importance, and that he has left an open door to a relationship with me. I was foolish to allow him to slip through my hands one time, and I will not be so unwise the next time. There will be a next time, honey, I can assure you."

Alivia's face heated as her eyes hurled fiery darts toward the loathsome woman. "May I inform you of my rodeo competition days? Steer roping was one of my favorite categories. If I could wrestle a steer to the ground, I could surely take you down." She took a step toward Selena with a fierce scowl. She snatched up Selena's purse and dumped everything out onto the floor, searching for the keys. She kept the whole key ring.

Alivia spoke with concentrated civility. "Get out of my home. Now. You are no longer welcome here. You have no reason to be here now or in the future. Get out."

With a look of alarm on her face, Selena went. She gave one last appeal before she exited the house. "I can't go anywhere without my keys."

With a smile of contempt, Alivia answered. "Sure, you can. You're a grown woman. Figure something out but do your thinking outside."

Alivia huffed her way to the kitchen for a drink of water. She couldn't remember a time that she had been so furious. Wow. What had happened to her usual placid disposition? It took her almost an hour to calm down.

She heard the doorbell ring, and with a deep sigh she went to answer the door. She hoped that woman was not ringing the bell. She opened the door and was shocked to see Pete.

"Pete. Hello. I'm a little surprised to see you."

Grinning, he said, "Yeah, I guess you are. I had to come and see you one last time before my wife and I leave for Japan." His smile disappeared. "I can't leave the country with the guilt that has me burdened down. I won't leave you with the impression that I don't love you. I do love you. You will always have a special place in my heart. My love for you is genuine, Alivia. But not in the same way as my wife. Do you understand?"

Alivia threw herself into his arms. "Yes, I understand, Pete. I feel the same about you. Go live your wonderful life. I am doing great, my friend."

As Pete turned to leave, Alivia called after him. "Pete, I will always love you too."

With a smile of joy, Alivia returned to the family room. She had another surprise waiting for her—her husband. "Dayne, hi. I didn't realize you were coming home at this time of day."

With barely controlled emotions he answered her. "No, I don't suppose you did know. I thought I would surprise you, but it seems I am redundant. Alivia, I have decided to let you go."

"What does that mean, Dayne?"

With a sorrowful face he said, "It means I am letting you go."

Staring at him she repeated his words. "You are letting me go. Are you firing me from my position as your wife? Is that what you mean Dayne?"

"Don't be ridiculous, Alivia. Of course I am not firing you. I am giving you your freedom."

Alivia felt that same temper bubble up again. She marched across the room to confront him, and with her index finger, peppered him in the chest with little sharp jabs. "Oh no you are not, mister. You bought me and I am a nonrefundable purchase. I'll have you know, Mr. Travers, that I am not a washing machine that you can bring home and try out and then return if it doesn't meet your expectations."

Dayne's temper flared quickly. "A man doesn't enjoy coming home and seeing his wife hugging another man and telling him she will always love him."

Huffing, Alivia answered with zest. "Neither does a wife like to come home and see another woman resting on the sofa, sipping coffee from a china cup. One who has entered with her own key. A key that was given to her by my own husband!"

Dayne's mouth dropped open. "What are you talking about?"

Alivia's finger came back out to punch her husband in the chest again. "Selena, that's who I'm talking about. She was inside this house when I came in. You gave her a key to this house. Can you deny that?"

After capturing her hands, Dayne answered, "I gave her a key when she was working with the interior designer. I allowed her to do as she pleased with the house because I thought at the time that she would become my wife. I never even thought to retrieve the key."

Alivia gazed around the room. "No wonder I hate this place. Look at it, Dayne. Look around you. All crystal and gold. It is flamboyant. There isn't a comfortable place to sit anywhere in this house." She was really wound up as she paced the room. "Look at this crystal bowl of geraniums. What is wrong with having real flowers with a pleasing fragrance?" She picked up the arrangement and hurled it at the wall.

All the angst and anger and disappointment of the past several months came to a head and exploded as molten lava spews from a volcano. Alivia gave up all control over her emotions as she went around the room with destruction in her heart and mind. She tore paintings from the wall and smashed several crystal objects that happened to be in her path. As suddenly as it started, the tantrum came to a halt.

Placing her hands over her face, she fell to the floor. "Oh, Dayne. I am so ashamed! I have never thrown such a tantrum in my entire life. I don't know what came over me. I beg forgiveness, if it is possible."

Grinning like an insane person, Dayne reached down to help her up. "Come, Alivia, allow me to help you off the floor."

Shaking her head she said, "No, Dayne. I can't face you. Not after what I have done. Please leave me alone for a few minutes, and I will get my stuff together and go back to Dad's place."

"Not a chance, sweetheart. Not now. Not ever. Don't you see what just happened?"

"Yes, I see. I had a giant temper fit."

"You are wrong, Alivia. Please get up so I can talk to you. What I see is a wife who is jealous of another woman. A woman of my past that means nothing to me. Alivia, you have exhibited all the signs of jealousy, and I couldn't be happier."

She looked at him in confusion. "You are happy that I lost all my self-control and threw a tantrum like a toddler?"

Laughing, he replied, "Absolutely. I take it to mean that you care for me. Maybe even love me?" He stood there with a silly grin plastered to his face.

She looked at him and realized that he was right. But she was not about to be the first to declare her love.

"Alivia, I love you. I have loved you for a long time."

"But we just recently met. How can you say that?"

"You don't remember, but we met over two years ago at an event. I was drawn by your absolute purity and goodness. I admit to you that your dad and I conspired together to come up with a solution of how to convince you to marry me."

"Wait a minute. Are you saying that Dad made false statements to me about his financial crisis? I can't believe my dad would lie to me like that for any reason."

"No, no. That is not what I mean at all. I mean that I confessed my love to your parents, and Kenneth really did need money. I merely showed him how we could both benefit from the financial difficulty. I talked to your mother at length and convinced her that I really do love you with all my heart. I wanted you for my wife, Alivia, and I admit to taking advantage of the situation to get you. Can you forgive me for being so selfish?"

Alivia reached up and pulled his head down to hers where she placed her lips against his. She finally admitted to herself her true feelings for her husband. Truth really does set one free. She reveled in the raw emotions and was unrestrained in her reaction to her husband's kiss. She was finally free to accept the pleasure of being in his arms with nothing holding her back. Alivia felt a deep satisfaction settle on her as she responded with her whole heart. When the intense kiss finally ended, she looked into his face to see a reflection of her smile on his face. How handsome this man she called husband was, and how his blue eyes sparkled and radiated happiness.

Dayne held Alivia in his arms and told her softly that she never had to enter this house again. "Sweetheart, I have heard of a ranch that just became available a few days ago. I'd like to take you out to look at it as a prospective home for us. If you don't want this place, we will look for another. If you want to move closer into Dallas, we will do so. We will live wherever you wish to live. It doesn't matter one iota to me as long as I am with you."

Alivia pulled herself from his embrace. "Dayne, you must not always allow me to have my way. That may turn me into a self-centered brat. I would like us to make these big decisions together."

Smiling, he answered, "I want to spoil you, Alivia. It gives me extreme pleasure to make you happy. But I promise that occasionally I will override your wishes if it is important to do so. For example, I will not allow you, not one more time, to get into your car and drive away from me without a full tank of gas."

Shuddering, she agreed wholeheartedly.

"By the way, will you tell me how you persuaded Selena to leave? I know she can be somewhat overbearing."

Alivia giggled and placed her hand over her mouth, eyes sparkling with mischief. "I merely told her about my rodeo days. It could be possible that I allowed her to think that I was good in the steer roping competition."

Dayne laughed with genuine amusement. "I wish I could have been there to see it. I can only imagine Selena's expression when you threatened her. I can see now that I had better be careful about making you angry with me. Oh yes, I have another quick question. Why was it significant to you that Selena was drinking from a china cup? I seem to recall that our guests always use those dishes."

"Exactly. You said the magic word—guests. She was not welcome here and had no right to use special china reserved for friends and family. Sorry. I guess that is another example of my unreasonable jealousy.

"I have a question for you, Dayne. How did you know that Pete and I weren't in love with each other? I didn't even realize it myself until recently."

Smiling, Dayne answered, "I knew from observation, Alivia, and on our wedding night when you confessed that you and Pete had never been intimate. I know for a fact that I could never spend years with you and not make love to you."

Alivia erased all mirth from her face as she confronted her husband. "Dayne, did I ever say the words 'I love you'? I do love you. I only realized it today after Natalie gave me a verbal lashing. I have not been honest with myself or you concerning my feelings. I confess that I tried not to love you, but my heart betrayed me. I have held you partly responsible for my mother's death. I convinced myself that the abduction was your fault because of your wealth. I know it makes no sense to you, but I was crushed that I never said goodbye to Mom. Can you find it in your heart to forgive me?"

Dayne listened as she went on to explain what had been revealed to her today. "I'm so sorry, Dayne. Please forgive me for hurting you and for being so stubborn."

Pulling her close, he whispered into her ear, "My darling Alivia, I hold no grudge against you for any of that stuff. I adore you completely and can't imagine myself being angry with you for over a minute at a time. Please don't fret about it. It is over and done. We have our whole lives before us. I'm sure that each of us will make our share of mistakes but know this; I will always love you and will try my very best to make you happy."

"Dayne, I wish it were possible to stay here forever."

"Oh? Have you changed your mind about moving?" He teased her, knowing she would take the bait.

"No! Absolutely not. I meant I wish I could live in your arms. Dayne Travers, you are bad! You knew what I meant."

Chuckling, he answered, "Of course I did. That is why I teased you. You are so easy to pick at, Alivia. I look forward to years of teasing you. Now that we have this settled, are you ready to view the property?"

Hand in hand they walked out and got into Dayne's vehicle together. They were both on a natural high as they made the forty-five-minute drive out into the country. Alivia was confused when they pulled up to her parents' house.

"I thought we were driving out to look at property to buy."

"We are there."

"I don't understand, Dayne. Are you buying this house?"

Dayne gazed at Alivia, eyes ablaze with love. "If you want to live here, yes, I am buying it. Kenneth told me this week that he would love to sell the ranch and move closer to town. He hates this long drive every day. He was willing to do it for Meagan's sake because she loved living on this ranch so much. He wants a smaller house with less maintenance. Are you interested?"

Alivia burst into tears. "I can't believe that you are being so kind, Dayne. I dearly love this place, but I can't be fully content if I know you had rather be somewhere else. This is one of those decisions that I mentioned earlier about making together. I won't accept such a sacrifice from you, Dayne."

"Alivia, it is no sacrifice for me to live here. We will do a little updating, leave it as is, or build another house to your specifications. Tell me what you want. If living here makes you feel close to your mother, then by all means let's move here."

Alivia flung herself into her husband's arms. "You have made me so happy, Dayne. What did I ever do to deserve you?"

Chapter 58

Dayne left Alivia and went back to town for a couple of hours. She took advantage of the time to make a couple of calls. Her first call was to Natalie. "Nat, thank you for straightening me out this morning. I was so angry at first and denied the accusations you threw at me. But Nat, I had a revelation! I remembered an incident from the hospital when I almost died. Mom came to me, Nat. She kissed me on the cheek and told me she had to go. I did get to tell her goodbye! That was the number one thing that has been bothering me.

"I also had to acknowledge my feelings for my husband. I found out quickly that I am a normal woman, Nat, when I got to Dayne's home and discovered his ex-fiancée there. I have never been so jealous in my life. I believe I could have snatched out every hair on her head! You would not have recognized your sister at that moment, Natalie. I went berserk."

Natalie gasped into the phone. "Did you fight her, Alivia? Did you attack her? That doesn't sound normal for you."

"You can believe that I wasn't normal, sister. I think I used extreme caution." Chuckling, she recounted the sequence of events to Natalie.

"What? Are you kidding me Alivia? Did you really throw her out without her car keys?"

"I did. I don't know how she left, but she did leave. I threw her keys into the trash bin."

They both laughed as they got a mental picture of Selena storming away with someone she called for help. "She got just what she deserved, Nat. She was up to no good. I think she changed her mind about wanting Dayne. But too late for her. He is taken."

"Tell me Alivia, did you tell Dayne what you did? Have you seen him today?"

"Yes and yes. We have everything all worked out, big sis. That is, we came to an agreement after my tantrum."

"Your what?"

"You heard correctly. I said tantrum. I went crazy on Dayne. He came in an hour or so after Selena left. He just happened to arrive as Pete was at the door. Dayne thought he was being magnanimous by letting me go. I laid into him, Nat. Just thinking about it gives me the shivers, but at the same time I want to laugh. He went into shock."

"Alivia, what did you do to him?"

"I punched him in the chest and destroyed several things in the family room. The funniest thing about it is that he was elated by my behavior. He said I showed all the signs of a jealous woman and his heart swelled in his chest seeing my demonstration. To him it meant I care for him."

Natalie took a minute to absorb the news from Alivia. "Did Dayne tell you that he loves you? Did you tell him?"

Dreamy eyed, Alivia answered her sister's questions. "Let me go for now, sister. I have to make another call."

Alivia took time to brew a pot of coffee before she called Morgan. From past experience she knew this call would be lengthy. Morgan always wanted details. She had to think of what she felt free to tell her. She didn't want the whole city to know she had developed a horrible temper.

Epilogue

ayne suggested an extended honeymoon on his yacht on the Mediterranean coast. They stopped to visit places she had never seen and spent countless days going nowhere. Alivia was bombarded with ideas for a series of children's books using Tootie and Tinker as the stars. She knew the boys would be excited about them.

They toured until they received word that all construction on the house was finished. They got to know each other and created a bond that would not be easily be broken. Both sailed through the days in contentment.

Alivia picked up some type of virus on the way home and felt terrible. She couldn't hold anything in her stomach and was always tired and sleepy. Dayne insisted that she see a doctor as soon as they docked.

After the examination the doctor asked them to follow him to his office. He looked across the desk at them and told them that the virus would last awhile longer. She was two months pregnant.

In shock they whipped their heads around to look each other in the face. Dayne's smile came out to dazzle her as he acknowledged what the doctor had said.

With an impish grin she asked, "You do realize that twins run in my family, right?"

www.ingramcontent.com/pod-product-compliance
Lightning Source LLC
Chambersburg PA
CBHW020406180626
46812CB00003B/860